OTHER BOOKS BY FRANK KING

Down and Dirty
Night Vision
Raya
Sleeping Dogs Die

FRANK KING

TAKE THE D TRAIN

E. P. DUTTON   NEW YORK

Published in the United States by E. P. Dutton,
a division of Penguin Books USA Inc.,
2 Park Avenue, New York, N.Y. 10016.

Published simultaneously in Canada by Fitzhenry and Whiteside, Limited, Toronto.

Library of Congress Cataloging-in-Publication Data
King, Frank, 1936–
Take the "D" train / Frank King.—1st ed.
p.   cm.
ISBN 0-525-24836-6
I. Title
PS3561.I4755T35   1990

813'.54—dc20

89-36200
CIP

1 3 5 7 9 10 8 6 4 2

First Edition

For that homeless woman on West 51st Street
who told me her dog had been kidnapped
by the Mayor

1

At six-thirty in the morning of that very cold Thursday in January, I was walking west on 51st Street toward Eleventh Avenue carrying a large pot and followed by my five dogs.

No doubt it was a very bizarre sight.

What was in the pot? Hot oatmeal.

Every morning I made a large pot of oatmeal for my dogs in which I threw assorted half-cooked pieces of muscle and organ meat along with chopped greens.

But that morning I made an extra pot and it was the extra pot that I was carrying.

To whom was I carrying that pot?

To a group of homeless alcoholic derelicts who lived on the abandoned half-sunken Penn Central tracks that lay like a transverse north/south scar on the skin of Hell's Kitchen.

Delivering oatmeal to homeless people was really not

one of my usual activities. I did do volunteer work a couple of times a week for the West Side League for the Homeless, but it really didn't involve oatmeal.

But that morning, it was so ferociously cold when I got up that I kept thinking of Charlie Seven, Mrs. Toast, Arthur, Sleepy, and Little Arthur—all huddled together under their cardboard tents. They were, I suppose, *my* homeless. I spent time with them. I brought them food and booze when I had the money. I tried to look out for them. And that morning, I just wanted them to have some hot oatmeal.

Actually, it wasn't too bright a move, but out-of-work actresses like myself have never been known to be bright. Fortitude is what we're about.

The dogs were quite happy. They rarely were all out together for a walk and the freezing weather invigorated them.

They were all with me. There was huge, gloomy Molson, and the matron, Budweiser, and prancing, inquisitive Heineken, and Stout, more frightened of the street than the apartment and trying to melt in the early morning darkness.

And there was Bernstein, not a stray mongrel like the others, who had been rescued from the street, but a full-blooded, magnificent German shepherd who had actually been rescued from a life of crime. He, Bernstein, heeled without a leash beside me.

The farther west I walked the more the freezing morning was laced with that strange bittersweet smell of smoke and burned wood and charred stone. It had been so far a very incendiary winter in Hell's Kitchen. The sound of fire engines was always heard. The abandoned buildings were being torched relentlessly. Hades was upon us.

I never reached the Penn Central tracks with my oatmeal.

Halfway between Tenth and Eleventh Avenues, Molson bolted past me into the shadow of a building line. It was very odd because Molson lived his life in slow motion.

The big dog's movement was so sudden and so unexpected that I reached out to grab him and lost control of the pot. It clanged and bounced onto the pavement, its contents splattering and immediately attacked by the dogs.

When I came upon Molson he was standing happily over Charlie Seven. The homeless man was calmly stretched out in the doorway, drinking foul-smelling wine from a small bottle wrapped in a tattered bag. From time to time Molson's enormous tongue splashed over the derelict's face.

No matter how many times I saw Charlie Seven, his appearance mesmerized me. He had lived on the street for a long time and he looked it. Tall, cadaverous, long-haired, long-bearded, his face and body a United Nations of sores. He looked as if he came from another age—from the Elizabethan underclass perhaps—groveling for dropped coins beneath the thick wooden planks of the Globe Theatre.

He didn't really wear clothes—he wrapped himself in whatever was at hand regardless of the weather. Charlie Seven was Rag Man.

He was, also, I realized, crazy. He was schizoid, paranoid, and probably about twenty other labels from the current edition of the American Psychiatric Association's *Diagnostic and Statistical Manual of Mental Disorders.*

One moment he knew me . . . he knew my name was Sally Tepper . . . he knew where I lived . . . he knew the names of my dogs . . . he knew what I liked to talk about.

The next moment he didn't know me at all.

One moment he talked rationally . . . the next moment he talked nonsense.

One moment he was totally submissive . . . the next moment he would cut your face open with a broken wine bottle.

In fact, the only dependable thing about him was his affection for Molson and Molson's affection for him. He once told me that Molson was his uncle. I told him that Molson was a dog—part mastiff, part wolfhound, part something else. I told him Molson was a big, goofy stray dog who couldn't be his uncle because his uncle would have to be human. Charlie Seven just grinned.

I didn't know where Charlie Seven came from or how he had gotten that crazy name. Why not Charlie Nine or Charlie Twelve? Nor did I know anything about his friends from the railroad tracks—Mrs. Toast and Sleepy and the others.

"Are you OK, Charlie?" I asked, trying to pull Molson away.

Charlie didn't answer me. He stared straight ahead. The smell coming from him was overpowering. I talked to him again. He didn't answer. It was no use. When Charlie Seven decided to remain silent, he remained silent. That's all.

I pulled Molson back to the sidewalk. The other dogs were on their haunches, staring at us, licking their chops after the unexpected treat of more oatmeal.

I picked up the pot. It had been licked clean. The mission of mercy had turned out to be futile.

Gathering the dogs and the pot I walked back home as the darkness lifted on the morning streets.

By the time I reached the house and climbed the stairs I felt as if I had been up for thirty-six straight hours.

What I saw taped onto my door didn't make me feel better.

It was an eviction notice.

2

This time, I knew, there would be no reprieve. The eviction notice, this time, meant eviction. Get out now. Leave. Vanish. Vacate. Extirpate thyself.

For six years I had fought the landlords and the tenants. Everyone wanted me out because I had five dogs and would take in any other stray dogs I found.

I spent so much time in Housing Court downtown that old Puerto Rican women thought I worked for the city. I had fought and won time after time.

But now, as Malcolm X once said, the chickens had come home to roost.

I had seventy-two hours.

I sat down in my apartment and cried. The dogs didn't know what was going on. The eviction notice lay on the floor in front of the sofa. Budweiser sniffed it. Finally, Bernstein lay down on it.

When my weepy depression lifted, I began to make phone calls. To anyone and everyone. Did they know of an apartment? Did they know of a sublet? I called people with whom my relationship was so vague that neither of us knew who was speaking to the other.

No one knew of an apartment. An empty apartment in Hell's Kitchen at a reasonable rental was as rare as a short order cook who knew how to scramble eggs correctly.

I mean, there were thousands of empty apartments, but the landlords wouldn't rent them—they were waiting for the inevitable co-oping.

There were hundreds of burned-out abandoned buildings, of course, but they didn't have running water. And there were all those thousands of remodeled apartments with stratospheric price tags. These, in fact, were so outside my financial possibilities that when I passed one in the street I felt as if I should genuflect.

By noon of that day I knew I wouldn't find an apartment. Not, at least, before I had to get out.

In the back of my head was the delicious desire to trash the apartment . . . to scrawl on the walls . . . to rip out the fixtures . . . but my Christian upbringing put a brake on that.

By three o'clock I had decided on a plan. In fact, I wrote the plan out on a new yellow legal pad on which I had been doodling for days—theatrical fantasies of an out-of-work actress. You know the kind—Olivier's agent calls me to do a new production of *The Prince and the Showgirl* with me in the Marilyn Monroe part.

I laid out the plan, outlined in sequence:

A. Get out of apartment now.
B. Leave everything. Everything. Like Jesus said: *Carry only one tunic.* Go out into the world with the dogs and one suitcase.
C. Put 3 dogs in kennel.
D. Take hotel room at weekly rate.
E. Sneak two remaining dogs into hotel.

F. Pray.

G. Look for an apartment and cashier's job.

For some reason, as if it were a profound document—like the Magna Carta—I signed my name with a flourish, *Sally Tepper*. And I even gave the last letter a vigorous curl.

And then I went into a two-hour agitated depression. I was so distraught that I emptied out the whole refrigerator and just let the dogs gorge themselves as their fancy took them from the menu lying on the floor. After all, they were losing their home, too.

What pulled me out of my funk was that wonderful Hell's Kitchen anti-depressant therapy—a freezing apartment. By five o'clock in the evening it was so cold the windowpanes were screaming.

Molson, however, did not mind the cold at all. The large beast was sitting placidly in front of the window, one paw on a mangled loaf of whole wheat bread, taking delicious bites from time to time while trying to spit out the cellophane he was taking in along with the nutrition.

"Molson," I said to him, "how can you eat at a time like this? Don't you understand we are being evicted?"

Molson groaned. But kept chewing.

The longer I waited, the worse it would be. Get out now, Sally, now.

So, at five-thirty in the afternoon of a day that had started with a spilled pot of charity oatmeal, I began the manic evacuation.

First I went to the cash machine and took out $300 cash—the most allowable in one withdrawal. That left me with $2,600 to my name. It wasn't much, but it was all I had been able to save from a succession of cashiering jobs in restaurants and small acting parts over the years. It was a lot more than a lot of people in Hell's Kitchen had.

I took a cab to Queens (knocking over three old ladies and two advertising executives to get it) and placed Heineken, Stout, and Molson in a kennel by a cemetery off Woodhaven Boulevard. They had been there before and they actually liked the lady who ran it. They only moaned a little as I left, standing together shoulder to shoulder in the large, wired-in run.

I took the subway back to Manhattan, rushed upstairs, changed into something presentable, and began cruising the neighborhood for a hotel with a weekly rate.

I started from the top out of perversity. From the Hilton to the Omni to the Edison to the Wellington. Down and down I went trying to escape from their insane rates.

Finally, exhausted, I found myself standing on the corner of 55th Street and Broadway staring at the venerable, decaying Woodward—a Single Room Occupancy joint.

Gerard Manley Hopkins' poem popped into my head—*It is the blight Man was born for/It is Margaret you mourn for . . .*

In my rendition I changed Margaret to Woodward.

Actually, the hotel was a neighborhood legend: one-third welfare cases; one-third released convicts; one-third busloads of Peruvian or other South American tourists.

I walked into the lobby. There was the smell of spilt milk. The Hispanic man behind the counter—he had snow-white hair—stared at me.

"Do you rent rooms by the week?" I asked.

He grinned. He was wearing a tiepin but no tie. He had a big moustache which was not white like his hair.

I had anticipated the grin. I mean, when a good-looking redhead walks into a dump like the Woodward for a room—the hooker gongs go off all over the hotel.

But the fact is I don't look like a hooker. I look like a Broadway showgirl. I'm five feet–nine inches tall and I have the kind of strong, large-boned body, long red hair—done up in braids—and freckled white skin that makes people, particularly tourists, think they saw me in a musical. And I surely don't dress like a hooker—when I'm not cashiering in winter I usually wear overalls and cashmere sweaters in an attempt to deaccentuate my unfortunate "voluptuousness."

Anyway, I was prepared for the response, so I said: "Father Demetrius recommended this place to me. I'm a secretary at the parish house on Forty-eighth Street."

He was so dazzled by my lie that he turned away as if he were inspecting a computerized list of vacancies.

"Three hundred forty-nine fifty per week. A hundred dollar deposit. No pets. No visitors. No cooking in rooms."

So, the deal was made. One tiny room on the third floor. Next to the hall bathroom.

Now came the hard part—to sneak the remaining dogs in and survive the first night.

First I rushed back to my apartment, grabbed the suitcase, rushed back to the hotel, and checked in.

I avoided the coffinlike elevator and took the stairs. I would use the stairs, I knew, to smuggle the beasts in.

The room was so small and so dingy and so damn down and out that I just stood in the center of the room in a state of shock for about a half hour.

Its only saving grace was that the single window was just under the huge neon sign of the hotel on the Broadway side. So every five seconds one would be illuminated by a purple glow.

I left the suitcase on the bed and returned to the apartment.

Budweiser and Bernstein knew something was up—they kept eyeing me suspiciously.

I sat down on the sofa. It had been rescued from the front of a burned-out building on 51st Street four or five years ago. A crazy old man on Eleventh Avenue had re-uphostered it for me for $59.95 in what seemed to be old pajama tops.

It dawned on me as I sat there that I had forgotten all about the change of address card that must be filed with the post office so that banks, insurance companies, utility

9

companies, relatives, and friends would know where I had gone.

But what was the forwarding address? The Woodward? Impossible.

First things first, I said, and then repeated it again and again—luxuriating in the cliché.

"Dogs," I said, "we are going to sneak in. Imagine you are starring in a remake of *The Guns of Navarone*. The Woodward is the gun emplacement. The desk clerk is the Gestapo. We are the good guys."

Bernstein did look a little like Gregory Peck.

I stood up. I realized that the moment I walked out this time I would never again step foot in the apartment as long as I lived.

It was indescribably sad.

I mean, how can one leave a place where one had slept all those years, and made love, and fed the dogs, and cried and laughed.

I mean, how many damn nights had I lain there, in that bed, and memorized lines from some dinky play in some dinky loft, while staring at the peeling plaster of the ceiling.

The map of the ceiling was in my head. Like the faces of my parents.

Well, the show must go on. How's that for a cliché! I also like "You can't go home again." Or how about—"Just because you're paranoid doesn't mean they aren't after you."

At 11:30 I walked out with the two dogs, carrying the last of my portable belongings in a shopping bag. I left the keys on the floor. I left the door open. And I silently uttered a specially pernicious curse upon the head of my landlord and the neighbors who filed nuisance charges against me and my dogs.

The assault on the fortress was about to begin.

Actually, it was over quickly.

I huddled in a doorway on the corner across from the hotel.

At about midnight a large group of South Americans returned from their adventures.

Waiting until they had jammed the lobby of the Woodward, and keeping Budweiser and Bernstein on a tight left-hand leash, I walked quickly through the lobby and up the stairs—the room clerk's vision totally blocked by the crush of tourists.

When we were all safely in the room, I fell onto the soft bed. The dogs jumped up beside me, confused.

We lay there. The neon light outside the window flicked on and off.

I thought that it had been the worst day of my life. I would soon find out how mistaken I had been.

3

Icannot even describe the lunacy of my first three days at the Hotel Woodward.

First, I realized how stupid I had been to leave the apartment without taking my pots and pans and linens. What had possessed me to abandon everything as if I was about to start a new life when all I was really doing was looking for a new apartment? But I couldn't go back. The bridges were burned. Let my neighbors have a garage sale with what remained in the apartment. They'd probably burn it all.

Second, the room next door was occupied by a young man who kept his door open three inches with the chain on. Whenever one passed, one saw him, sitting, staring, silent. He was probably, I thought, a recently released inmate from some state hospital for the criminally insane. He was so spooky I began to fantasize that he was plotting to cook one of my dogs.

And most of all, there was the constant slinking down-stairs, scheming how to smuggle the dogs in and out for walks, begging them to keep their jaws shut so no one would report wild beasts in one of the rooms.

Twice a day, at various times, one human and two canine criminals shivered against the wall, waiting, watching, ready to dash in and out.

One time they caught me coming in with the dogs. The desk clerk roared. I told him I was walking the dogs for a rich old woman who lived on 57th Street and Seventh Avenue. I told him I had to go up to my room for a minute because I had forgotten an important letter that had to be mailed. Would he watch the dogs for me? He pondered my question nervously. He stared at Bernstein, who was curling his lip at him. Then he let me take them up. I don't know what he thought when I didn't come down.

Sometimes I would just hang around the lobby alone and wait until the desk clerk was busy, then run upstairs and smuggle them out. On and on it went, subterfuge, duplicity, theater!

By the end of the third day I realized that I hadn't made a single apartment or job inquiry. The criminal enterprise was consuming all my energy.

On the fourth day, in the afternoon, I went out to Queens to visit my three other dogs in the kennel.

It was a freezing cold day with bright sunlight. I spent four hours in the run with them, listening to their complaints, feeding them chunks of muenster cheese with caraway seeds, and scratching them.

They never looked so good, because for the first time in years they were spending most of their days outdoors. Even huge, sleepwalking Molson broke into a trot once in a while.

The woman who ran the kennel told me they were doing fine but they tended to howl at night. Considering the kennel was situated next to a graveyard, I told her, it might be considered an appropriate response.

By the time I got back to the city it was late and dark. I needed a break . . . a rest . . . a sense of calm.

So, for the first time in months, I went to Amy's—the bar on Ninth Avenue and 55th Street. It hadn't changed. Same old bar, same old mix of cops and actors and hustlers and church ladies . . . a Hell's Kitchen bar.

The bartender remembered me, drawing an ale before I opened my mouth. But why shouldn't he? When I was going with Jack Troy I used to be in Amy's twice a day, every day.

"Where've you been?" He asked.

"Meditating."

"I love women who meditate, " he replied.

"I thought you told me you loved all women."

"None more than you," he said, laughing, but serious, on the make, as all ex-actors who turned bartenders invariably are.

He leaned over the bar staring at my body. I took the ale and went to a booth. The bartender was an ass, but he didn't bother me; I had been around too long.

It was so nice sitting there in the half darkness—a single lamp at each table. Conversations drifted across the bar and to the booths. The place gradually began to fill as the evening progressed.

I had another ale, and another.

If I left I would have to go back to the Woodward and sneak the dogs out and in again.

It was odd sitting there now. It had never occurred to me, some six years previously, when I had my first ale at Amy's, that my situation would not have changed at all. I mean, I was too good an actress. I was going to make it. I was going to have a high-priced, high-floor studio apartment on 58th and Seventh, or in the Beresford.

Of course, I had made it, humanely. I had survived. I had fought. I had kept my sanity and my principles and my perspective and my compassion. The parts, alas, had eluded me.

The ale made me kindly and sleepy. It had been a long day and Queens was very cold. I drifted off. It wasn't sleep. It was a kind of fatigue. The dark panels of Amy's walls seemed to soothe me, to relieve everything.

A sudden jerk of my arm snapped me out of it.

I opened my eyes and recoiled in fear at a fat woman, who seemed to be attacking me.

Then I realized it was only Beth White.

She dropped into the seat across from me. Her hair was pulled back. Her face was red from the cold. She was wearing her usual enormous overalls and sweater upon sweater. Her hands were puffed and stiff.

Beth White and Robert Allissandro were co-directors of the West Side League for the Homeless. They were both ex-religious. They had both left their orders in the turmoil following Vatican II to go among the "people." And they had done so. Bravely, doggedly, often pathetically, they kept the League alive, scrounging money from any and all sources—providing food, legal services, prayers, clothing, and God knows what else for the homeless.

Beth White was one of those hard/soft women who seemed to appear only among ex-nuns. Nothing fazed her . . . nothing was impossible for her . . . nothing could stop her from her mission to somehow in some way increase the amount of love in the world.

When I first met her we used to talk a lot. About foolish things. Once she assured me that all dogs go to heaven and once there miraculously acquire human speech so they can converse rationally with their ex-masters.

"Beth," I exhaled.

"Don't 'Beth' me, " she growled. "Where the hell have you been? I've been looking for you. People have been looking for you. You just vanished."

"I was evicted."

"I know you were evicted. So what? Where are you staying? Why didn't you come to the office and tell us you're OK? What's the matter with your senses, Sally?"

She reached across the table and appropriated what was left of my ale.

"I checked into the Woodward on Fifty-fifth and Broadway."

"God, not the Woodward!"

"I didn't have too many options," I said.

She nodded suddenly and her eyes filled with tears.

"C'mon, Beth," I said, "the Woodward is not *that* bad."

"Charlie Seven is dead." Beth spoke the words carefully, as if she were reciting something.

I sat back so hard my head banged into the booth.

"What are you talking about, Beth? I just saw him a few days ago. Molson found him. In an alley. I was bringing them oatmeal."

"He was murdered, Sally. In the subway station at Rockefeller Center. They hung him from the top of the token booth."

I stared at her. I could not move or speak.

She finished the ale. Her hands were clasped now, hard.

"It's horrible, Sally. They found him hanging there and someone had stuffed a rolled-up hundred dollar bill into his ear."

She left the table and quickly came back with two ales and a brandy.

"They don't know who did it. It was probably some crazy kids from Forty-second Street. And probably a drunk tourist saw him hanging there and stuffed the bill into his ear. Poor Charlie. Oh, Sally, I'm sorry."

I didn't cry. I just laid my head down on my arms and stared at the stem of the brandy glass.

"I'll look for an apartment for you, Sally," she said. Then she added: "Do you need money?"

I didn't answer. She stood up.

"Do you want me to take you back to your hotel?"

I didn't answer.

She reached into her back pocket and brought out two

envelopes that she dropped on the table in front of me.

"People have been leaving mail for you at the League office," she said. She grasped my hands tightly. She kissed me on the head. Then she was gone.

I picked up one of the envelopes. It was a filthy and crumpled manila thing.

I ripped it open.

Two tiny sewing packets fell out. They were the kind you buy in Woolworth's before you go on a trip.

A small piece of cardboard fell out with them.

On it was printed: MERY CHRIMAX. CHARLE

It was a Christmas gift from Charlie Seven. He must have dropped it off at the League office the day before he was murdered.

Poor Charlie! Didn't he know Christmas was a month past?

And then I started to cry. I stuffed the napkin into my mouth. Why Charlie Seven? Why the lowest and the poorest and the craziest? I had to get out of there. I had to stop weeping. But I couldn't move. The sewing packets were like grotesque coffin ornaments; each one with multicolored threads wrapped around a cardboard spindle and tiny needles.

I think I finally fell asleep then, in the booth. When I awoke the clock over the bar read 11:45 P.M.

I sipped the brandy and shoveled the sewing packets and the note back into the envelope.

The other letter still lay on the table.

I opened it. It was a note:

Dear Miss Tepper:
I am truly sorry that it was necessary to proceed with the eviction. Would you please come up to my office at your earliest convenience? I assure you it will be worth the effort.
                              Sincerely,
                              Stephen Patrice

17

I read it by the dim light, in a kind of bewildered astonishment.

Stephen Patrice was my landlord. He had been trying to evict me for years. He had finally succeeded. He was the enemy. Whatever had possessed him to write to me? I would as soon visit his office as paint my toenails.

I sat back, bitter. Why hadn't it been him? Why hadn't someone hung the rich and powerful Mr. Patrice? Why Charlie Seven?

4

Why did I go up and see Stephen Patrice the next morning at his office on 41st Street and Madison Avenue?

I don't really know.

I think it had to do with the shock I felt from Charlie Seven's murder.

I wanted to confront something or someone visibly evil. And my landlord, I believed, was surely that. He represented everything I hated. He represented torn down theaters and bodegas . . . eviction . . . homelessness . . . futility . . . death . . . stray dogs and stray people . . . apple pie with maggots.

I dressed out of my suitcase as if I were going on some kind of dangerous mission—wool ski hat, ugly heavy sweater, turtleneck, heavy boots, no makeup at all.

By the time I reached 41st and Fifth I was beginning to have second thoughts. His letter had been apologetic.

Did I really want an apology? And what was the point of going up to his office to scream at him? Actually, I had never even spoken to him. In fact, I had seen him only once, in the housing court, surrounded by his entourage— lawyers, accountants, agents, manipulators.

Sure, I knew who Stephen Patrice was. He had a reputation for keeping a foot in both worlds. He was a slumlord. And at the same time he was a patron of the arts, a fervent supporter of the Landmarks Commission. A typical hypocrite.

But it was too cold to be indecisive. I went up. A male secretary asked my business. I told him I wanted to see Patrice. He asked me if I had an appointment. I produced the letter, holding it between my fingers as if it were infected.

The secretary vanished into an office with the letter. He quickly appeared again, in the doorway, holding the door open and waiting for me. I walked inside.

Patrice was at his very large, very empty modern desk. It was shaped like a kidney.

The room itself was small with no furniture except for the desk and two chairs. A small computer was on a wall stand. The walls were white. On them were a number of watercolors of New York bridges.

I was nervous and confused. I sat down.

He looked like a race car driver: short and slim, with black hair and moustache streaked with gray. He was wearing a white shirt open at the collar. He was a handsome man.

There was silence. Then he placed his palms on the desk and said: "Thank you for coming. I am very sorry that this mess had to happen."

"Then cry a little," I snapped, sarcastically.

His eyes flashed anger. He composed himself.

"You left me no choice, Miss Tepper. One dog, fine. Two dogs, why not? But you can't live in a building like that with five stray dogs. You asked for it. The tenants in your building were bombarding the agent for years to get you out."

"I see," I said. "You really love dogs. You were really my only friend in the building. You were really forced to evict me. You're really a kind, benevolent landlord. You're really a compassionate man—not a shark. God, what hypocrites you people are."

"Who is 'you people,' Miss Tepper?" He asked, leaning back in his chair.

"Hustlers. Developers. Sharks. Co-opers. Manipulators. You know who."

"I'm a real estate developer," he said, as if he were speaking to a child. "I have a vision of this area. I have a dream for it—a different kind of place. Theaters. Schools. Safe streets. And—"

"And millions of dollars in each of your bottomless pockets," I interrupted. I was trembling.

There was silence again.

He said: "You know, I've seen you several times."

"Not to my knowledge," I replied.

"You used to work as a cashier in that steakhouse on Forty-sixth and Ninth."

"I've worked in many places."

"It's not a piece of cake," he noted.

"What's not a piece of cake?"

"Trying to be an actress."

"I *am* an actress," I replied. His voice, I noted, changed often. Sometimes he sounded like a professor of urban planning. Sometime he sounded like a Hell's Kitchen stevedore.

Poor Charlie Seven, I thought, hung up like a piece of meat while Stephen Patrice weaves his futuristic net in safety behind his six-thousand-dollar desk and on the backs of us all.

My anger at the unfairness of it all so overwhelmed me that I thought fleetingly of trying to hurt Patrice, physically, in some way . . . any way. Then it passed.

21

"Would you have dinner with me some evening?" he asked.

"Have dinner with you?" I was astonished. I couldn't believe what I was hearing.

"Yes. I always liked you from a distance. I thought perhaps we could get to know each other better."

My god! He actually believed that I would go out with him!

I stared at him as if he were a very large roach. I reached across the desk, picked up the letter he had sent me and which the secretary had placed there, tore it to pieces, and flung it at him. He didn't move.

I turned and started to walk out.

"Miss Tepper. That's not why I asked you to come here."

I kept walking.

"I'm sorry I insulted you. Let's get down to business, then. I want to give you and your dogs an apartment in one of my buildings."

The only thing that could stop me from walking out was precisely what he'd said: the word "apartment."

"I want to make up for all the trouble I've caused you. You know, I've picked up a few strays myself."

To incinerate them, I thought. But I did stop walking. It is truly strange how quickly one's own survival overwhelms one's own conscience. An apartment!

5

Within twenty-four hours after my visit to Patrice's office I was sitting regally in my new abode, surrounded by my five dogs.

They had never been in such a luxurious space. It was a huge empty loft over a boiler repair shop on West 51st Street, between Tenth and Eleventh Avenues.

It was like being in a roller rink. There were twenty-four large filthy windows—four or five of them stuffed with cardboard.

The high ceiling was covered with hissing and dripping pipes.

There were five or six large empty crates on the floor and nothing else.

A small kitchen alcove contained a refrigerator and what appeared to be a stove, with several rows of high cabinets.

The bathroom was enormous and had never been renovated for apartment living: three toilets, three showers, and five sinks. There were no real closets, but there were large enclosed spaces at each end of the loft which seemed to have functioned at one time as storerooms or small offices—and each one spacious enough to happily contain an African elephant.

The rent was an unbelievably low $606.56 a month, Rent Stabilized, and the janitor, who had let me in and who lived across the street, had left a two-year lease on one of the crates, already signed by Patrice.

When another twenty-four hours had passed, I had purchased a mattress, bowls for the dogs, dog food, a mop and broom, a bucket, toilet articles, oatmeal, coffee, and eggs.

When another twenty-four hours had passed I had put my name on the mailbox, filled out a change-of-address card at the post office, contracted for a phone, turned on the electricity and the gas, bought towels and a frying pan and a tea kettle and three mugs and aspirin.

Three thrift stores on Ninth Avenue were the source of my purchases. They were like Third World supermarkets. No one spoke English.

And then I rested.

When I awoke after my third night in the loft, I sat up on my mattress and just grinned as the sunlight poured through the windows.

The overhead pipes hissed with steam, battling the cold drafts that still came through the cardboard-stuffed windows.

The dogs were scattered throughout the loft, catching the sun.

All except Heineken.

He was chewing something and growling.

My well-being vanished. A mouse? A rat? A poor bird? Who knew what creatures lived in this building.

I called Heineken's name. He growled and turned away.

I yelled at him. He got up and trotted farther away from me.

Finally, I leaped from the mattress and cornered him under a window.

He growled again. I whacked him on the rump. He dropped what he was chewing and ran to the matron, Budweiser, for protection. All the dogs began to bark at me in protest.

I stared at the object on the floor.

It was one of the sewing packets Charlie had sent me, just before he was murdered.

I had forgotten all about the gift.

What a bad friend I had been. The anxiety over getting an apartment had overwhelmed everything.

I hadn't even found out what really happened.

I hadn't gone over to the Penn Central tracks to see if the rest of his homeless family was OK.

I hadn't done a damn thing except worry about poor little Sally Tepper.

The small packet was thoroughly drenched. The threads were ripped and mixed, the cardboard spool destroyed. Poor, wonderful, crazy Charlie Seven. His head so scattered by booze and cold and the street that he didn't even know when Christmas was. Maybe, I thought, when he saw all those Santa Clauses on the corners during the Christmas season ringing their bells he thought they were peddlers.

I closed my eyes and rocked on my heels. I could see Charlie in my mind. I could see him muttering with his ever present wine bottle wrapped in a paper bag. I could see him speaking to his "uncle"—to Molson.

I stared at the big dog. He stared back at me.

Be a friend in death, I thought. How? Bloody how?

"What can I do?" I asked Molson, suddenly confused and angry and impotent.

He just stared. I started to explain to him that the world was often ugly. Some live, some die. I told Molson to remember that it was only sheer coincidence that I had saved him that time by the 52nd Street pier. It was by chance that I was walking there—that I saw him.

What the hell could I do? Charlie Seven was dead. Why, in fact, did I feel that I must do something? He lived the kind of life that invited violent death. Did he have an option? I did what I could.

What? Bring him hot oatmeal?

Was Molson chastising me with his stare? Or was I hallucinating? Had Molson also believed that he was Charlie Seven's uncle?

There was, I realized, nothing I could do except find out what really had happened to Charlie.

I dressed slowly, aware of the absurdity, yet reluctant to give it up.

An hour later, I entered the cavernous, multilayered subway station of Rockefeller Center that runs between 47th and 50th Streets beneath Sixth Avenue.

At least ten token booths were scattered throughout the station; some in use, some shut down. All I knew was that Charlie Seven had been crucified on one of them.

I meandered back and forth through the station looking for transit cops. It felt strange. I mean, over the years I've had all kinds of bad dealings with regular NYPD cops, because in Hell's Kitchen they essentially work for the landlords, through no fault of their own. But I had never talked to a transit cop in my life.

The first one I cornered was wearing a name plate that read THIBEAU. He looked and dressed just like an NYPD cop except for the patch on his arm. He didn't know a thing.

The second one was a black cop with a name plate that read RALSTON. He didn't know a thing.

The third one was named MORAN. He was short and

stocky and light-haired and wasn't handling the cold too well. He kept blowing into his hands.

"I'm trying to find out about a murder that happened in the station last week."

He looked me up and down in a quizzical sort of sexual manner and asked: "Who are you?"

"The Ghost of Christmas Past," I said.

He didn't appreciate my quip. He stared past me.

"He was a friend of mine," I said.

"You mean the derelict?"

"Right."

He grinned at me wickedly. He figured I was either a kook, a writer, or a do-gooder—and none of those options appealed to him.

"Were you the one who found him?" I asked.

"No," he said.

"But you know about it?"

"Sure. Rieback found him."

"Where can I find Rieback?"

"He took some vacation time."

"I want to know what happened."

"Whattya mean? The guy was hung up on the top of a token booth. That's what happened. He was hung. He was executed by hanging. Like in the Westerns. Rieback cut him down. He found a hundred dollar bill stuffed into his ear. That's what happened."

"Did anyone see it happen?"

"Not that we know."

"No one?"

"No one."

"Does anyone know who did it? Does anyone have an idea?"

"No. Look, lady, whoever you are, in the last couple of months a whole slew of derelicts have gone down in the subways—hung, torched, stabbed, you name it. I mean, it has been open season on bums. So, your friend was another one. I'm sorry. What can I say? Dead derelicts aren't exactly our number one priority."

"What is?"

"I don't get you."

"What *is* your number one priority?" I asked, sarcastically.

He sighed as if I were profoundly stupid.

"Maybe, maybe, in a couple of months," he said, "some zonked out kids will get busted and drop a word or two about a bum that got hung on a token booth . . . maybe."

The sounds of the subway began to churn in my ears. A train pulled in. I heard yells. I saw kids racing for a token booth. I heard a train pull out. I heard the groaning, grinding, hissing sound of rails and tracks and switches and doors.

"Which token booth was it?" I asked.

"Rieback didn't tell me."

What was the last sound Charlie Seven heard? A train pulling into the station?

"I'm sorry about your friend," the transit cop Moran said, and started to walk away. Then he turned back.

"There was one funny thing Rieback told me. He said the guy was wearing a white shirt . . . a strange kind of tattered white shirt under his clothes. It had some fringes."

"Charlie Seven never wore a white shirt in his life," I replied.

"I'm telling you what Rieback told me, lady. He also said there was a weird design on the shirt—like a buffalo head."

Another train thundered through. Moran had said many derelicts had gone down. Had they all died to the sound of the wheels? Had they all heard the exact same thing before they died? Who was this transit cop? Was he making it all up? Was there really an epidemic of grotesque, anonymous no-one-gives-a-damn murders?

"Charlie Seven never had a white shirt in his life," I angrily repeated, adding, "with or without a buffalo on it."

"Any way you want it, lady," Moran said cynically, and sauntered off with a why-waste-time-on-fools look on his face.

I leaned against a cold wall of subway tiles. What had the cop said? *Dead derelicts are not a number one priority.* It seemed suddenly funny to me. What about live derelicts? Who was crazy in this city?

6

When I got back to my new loft it was past eleven. I walked the dogs and then resumed my cleaning, concentrating on scraping the filth off the windows. Actually, the only reason I started cleaning was that I didn't want to do what I had to do—go over to the Penn Central tracks and see how Charlie Seven's family was . . . find out from them what they thought really happened to Charlie . . . talk to Mrs. Toast, Sleepy, Arthur, and Little Arthur.

At noon my new phone rang. It was a very gentle sound in that very large space.

The caller was Stephen Patrice.

He wanted to know if I liked my new apartment.

I told him I was delighted with it. He said: "We're even now."

Then he wondered whether I would have dinner with him, at Cheval, a small French restaurant on Eighth Avenue that I'd always loved. How did he know I loved it?

I refused his offer, letting him know not so gently that the only obligation I had to him was to pay the rent.

He ignored my comments. He said: "You know, I don't want your enmity. I want your friendship."

"Time heals all wounds," I replied, and hung up.

Poor Patrice, I mused. Did he think getting me an apartment would persuade me to see him? Out of gratitude? Out of obligation? Did he really think I gave out sexual or any other favors for a price?

Finally, I did what I had to do. I took two of the dogs, Bernstein and Molson, and started out to find the family. It was a dangerous place they lived in and I never went there without at least two of the dogs accompanying me, preferably my largest ones.

En route, I purchased two bottles of cheap sweet wine, one small bottle of blackberry brandy, two ham and cheese sandwiches, and a box of chocolate-covered donuts.

We approached the old "right of way" through 49th Street, one of the many streets where it exists as a deep open trench, the tracks long ripped away, about thirty feet below street level, with treacherous garbage-strewn slopes. One could theoretically walk the entire north-south right of way—through the abandoned tunnels, out in the light for a block or two, and then underground again. But no one I knew ever did it. The right of way was now home to hundreds of stray dogs, stray cats, stray people—including many crazies.

It was truly a subterranean city. At night, in the winter, one could stand at street level and stare down at the fires that had been built by the homeless.

Holding Bernstein's and Molson's leashes with one hand, and the groceries with the other, I slithered down the mud-and-ice-crusted path to their home.

Halfway down I knew something was wrong. I braked.

The cardboard containers and packing cases they always slept in were gone.

Crazy Mrs. Toast's shopping cart was gone, along with the bizarre grill on which she was always roasting pieces of bread and distributing it with the words: "Eat toast. Want toast? Eat toast."

They were all gone, with their pathetic belongings. The space they had occupied for years was bare, except for the omnipresent windblown trash.

I started to clamber up the slope, frightened by the solitude . . . frightened by their absence. I stopped. A few yards away, lying on the slope under a large piece of filthy plastic was an old black man.

"Where are they?" I shouted at him, pointing below, the wind now beginning to howl.

The black man stared at me and didn't answer. His eyes were yellowish.

"Where did they go?" I asked him.

He didn't answer. I climbed up the slope and began to walk along the transverse, looking for them uptown and downtown. They had vanished.

Walking back, I let the bag of wine, sandwiches, and donuts roll down the slope where the black man was lying. He opened the paper bag slowly with cold-stiffened fingers and began to unscrew the top of the wine bottle.

Where could they be? They had lived here for years. They never went into a shelter. Sometimes during storms, they went to abandoned buildings. But they always left some of their belongings to mark the place.

I started to walk to the League office on Tenth Avenue. Beth White or Robert Allissandro would know what had happened to them, if anyone did.

It was getting colder and windier and darker. My arms were beginning to ache from holding the two dogs who were, in their fashion, becoming obstreperous.

The League office was located in the basement of an ancient three-story red building; the street level was occupied by a hardware store. When I entered, Beth and Robert were huddled over a portable heater. The office was, as usual, brightly lit. Five or six homeless people dozed in chairs. Stacks of papers and books and clothes and canned goods lined the peeling walls. Large crayon pictures done by children were taped above them.

Beth waved and gestured me over. I shook hands with Allissandro, a short, dark, slender man who moved like a dancer. He was, as usual, leery of my dogs. He was wearing a pea jacket and a wool cap. He looked dwarfed by Beth.

"Charlie Seven's family is gone. They vanished. All of them," I reported.

Beth seemed to disregard what I said.

"Didn't you hear me, Beth?" I asked angrily.

"I heard. But you have it wrong, Sally. Not all of them have vanished."

I didn't understand what she was getting at. The dogs plopped down on the floor. Bernstein yawned. Molson stepped on him. Bernstein growled. Molson averted his eyes, submissively.

"Little Arthur hasn't vanished. We know where he is. In the morgue. He killed himself. He dropped in front of a train last night in the Columbus Circle subway station. Or somebody pushed him."

I closed my eyes.

Little Arthur was truly little; he had lost both legs in some kind of industrial accident or some war—no one really knew. He got around on one of those platforms with roller skate wheels attached, using his arms as oars. He survived by begging. He was a violent, brooding, alcoholic derelict and only Charlie Seven could really control him. One always heard Little Arthur before one saw him; the platform on skates made a distinctive noise.

"We don't know where the others are," Allissandro added.

They offered me coffee. I refused. They offered me a chair. I refused. I dragged the dogs back out into the cold and went back to the loft. Once inside, I lay down on the mattress and fell asleep instantly.

The phone woke me. I looked at the clock. It was six.

Stephen Patrice was on the phone again. He wondered if I had changed my mind about having dinner with him at Cheval.

"Sure," I said, "anytime you want to walk my dogs, I'll have dinner with you."

There was a pause; then he slammed down the phone. "Good riddance to bad rubbish," I whispered—my grandmother's phrase. Then I made a cup of hot, sweet, black instant coffee.

Was it possible, I thought, as I paced the loft, followed by Stout and Heineken, who obviously thought it was some kind of game, was it possible that the transit cop had been right?

Had there really been a silent epidemic of killings beneath the city, the victims homeless?

Had Charlie Seven and Little Arthur been victims of that epidemic?

Who had used the word "epidemic" first—the transit cop or me? It was such a stupid word to use for murder. Murder isn't an airborne virus.

Someone started to knock at the door. All five dogs flew to it, barking.

I heard the super's voice, the one who lived across the street. I drove the dogs back and opened the door.

Next to the super stood Stephen Patrice. He smiled at me.

"Do I have to bring my own leash?" he asked.

I stepped back. It was unbelievable.

But he did it. I gave him the leashes. And he left to walk all five dogs at one time.

When he came back he stood in the doorway and said: "Well, I did my part of the bargain. Now you pay off."

We went to Cheval.

It had been months since I had worked, much less eaten, in a nice restaurant. And Cheval had always been

34

one of my favorites. It was one of those rare, reasonably priced, friendly neighborhood French restaurants.

At first I was angry and uncomfortable and silent. Patrice had outfoxed me to get me there and I was determined to make him pay for it.

But soon the good wine and the atmosphere and the warmth began to dissolve my anger. Patrice hardly had said a word, until I ordered sweetbreads for the main dish.

"I am too aggressive," he said, "always have been. And I apologize for that character flaw."

"How did you like walking five dogs?"

He laughed. I noticed that he had not touched his salad or the bread or the wine.

"I didn't like picking up after them."

"It's the law."

"So I understand."

"What did you think of Molson?"

"The big one? He's very slow."

"Many of us are."

"I can't imagine him as a stray."

"He was a stray. I found him on the West Fifty-second Street pier. He was about to commit suicide."

"I didn't know dogs kill themselves."

"You don't know a lot of things, Mr. Patrice."

"My friends call me just Patrice," he noted.

"I'm not your friend."

"Yes, I know. We're enemies. But I want to change that." He drank some wine.

Then he said: "You know I once invested in a Broadway show—a comedy. I lost a lot of money."

"There are eight million tragedies in the naked city," I retorted.

My sarcasm infuriated him for the first time.

"You know," he barked, "I love Hell's Kitchen as much as you do. More than you."

"Like you love Charlie Seven and Little Arthur."

He stared at me, perplexed.

"I don't know who you're talking about. I don't know those names."

"They're homeless derelicts who were murdered. They were my friends."

"But that's what I'm trying to do . . . make Hell's Kitchen safe . . . for everyone."

"Sure you are," I laughed at him, "with your condos and your atriums and your restaurants and your Bentleys. You're going to make it very safe for the rich."

The waitress came with the sweetbreads. Patrice had ordered veal.

Suddenly I had lost my appetite.

"I think that when you get to know me better you won't be so harsh in your judgment," he said quietly.

"What makes you think I'm going to get to know you better? What makes you think I'll ever see you again?"

"I love you," he said.

It was such a lunatic thing to say. It was so bizarre. I didn't know how to respond. I pushed the chair back and stared around, as if seeking help.

Finally, I said: "You love me? Listen, Mr. Landlord, I don't think you have any grasp of the word. Anyway, I thought hotshot developers like you get your love from five-hundred-dollar-a-night hookers. They're more your style."

He didn't respond. He picked at his veal morosely with his fork. He was close to fifty, but just then he looked like a child.

I heard a rumbling . . . a slight rumbling that seemed to come from the bowels of the restaurant. Then I realized it was the subway beneath us. I was suddenly ashamed to be sitting in that lovely restaurant while the homeless were being murdered. I suddenly could not justify my sweetbreads in the face of Charlie Seven's and Little Arthur's corpses.

"You look ill," he whispered gently, "let me take you home."

36

7

The next day he sent flowers and, along with them, an enormous plastic garbage bag filled with bones hung with slivers of meat. The flowers I assumed were for me and the bones for the dogs.

Just before noon, Beth called. She said a homeless woman had been torched to death by a youth gang on the old West Side Highway. She had thought at first it was Mrs. Toast—but it wasn't. No one seemed to know anything about the whereabouts of the rest of Charlie Seven's family.

I sat down and stared at Patrice's flowers.

It was like there was a hole in Hell's Kitchen and people were being pulled into it.

I looked around at my new home, at the dogs who were lolling in the sun that streamed wondrously through the enormous windows.

I had to look for work. I had to get back to acting

class. I had to buy furniture. I had to find Charlie's family.

What was I waiting for?

The phone rang again as I was scratching Budweiser between the ears. It was Patrice.

Was that what I was waiting for?

He said that he had business up around the Museum of Natural History. Would I like to take a ride with him . . . sit in the car while he double-parked . . . and then go stare at the Blue Whale that hung in all its enormousness between floors in the museum?

I didn't answer for a long time. I looked at Molson, who was on his back, his huge feet in the air. Was that Charlie Seven's face in his paw? Why had I been waiting for Patrice's call?

"Yes," I said.

I waited for him downstairs wearing the worst possible winter throw-ons I could muster. It was cold. The wind swept up my block from the river. I looked up, squinting in the sun. Five different dogs stared down at me from five different windows.

I waved at them. They didn't wave back.

Patrice pulled up in an old station wagon; the rear was filled with cartons.

"Where's your Mercedes?" I asked, sarcastically.

"It's being perfumed," he said, and opened the side door. I climbed in beside him.

We sat in the car for a while without moving or speaking. I suddenly realized we were both nervous.

It was a remembered nervousness: I had gone through it before; it was the nervousness of a teenager out for romance. God, how could that be! People were falling through holes to oblivion and I was . . . what? About to jump into bed with a shark?

I turned and looked at him. His face was contorted as if he were trying to speak but couldn't. I restrained a sudden urge to stroke the side of his head.

He started the car moving . . . uptown.

"When was the last time you were in the museum?" he asked.

"Years ago," I replied. I could see that he was sweating. I touched my forehead. No, I wasn't sweating. But I was warm. Our nervousness was disabling us. I opened a window and cold air blew through the car.

He suddenly went into a long reminiscence about his childhood and museums. I listened but didn't hear.

We pulled up in front of a building on 71st Street, west of Broadway. I waited in the car while he went in. He was wearing a faded mechanic's jumpsuit with an expensive cashmere sweater over it. He climbed the steps and then turned toward the car and waved. Then he laughed.

When he returned he brought a chocolate bar with him. We shared it in the freezing car. It was such a stupid thing to do. I mean, hotshot developers like Patrice simply don't lunch on chocolate bars.

Then we went to the Museum of Natural History and stared at the massive replica of the Blue Whale.

Suddenly, for no reason at all, I started to talk to Stephen Patrice about acting . . . about theater . . . about Sally Tepper the actress.

Right there—by the Blue Whale—I told him about the life . . . about how I almost made it but didn't . . . about the parts I had and the parts I missed . . . about my physical handicaps—too tall, too voluptuous . . . about my love for a wooden stage . . . about how it was the life I loved now and not the parts I would never get—the acting classes, the cashiering jobs, the hustle, the lies, the friends that come and go, the city.

I told him that all we had was theater. It was around us, in us. It was what kept us alive.

The more I talked, the more romantic and absurd I became. When I finally finished I was exhausted and not a little embarrassed.

Patrice took my arm and we walked to the cavernous museum coffee shop, sat down across from one another,

39

and made little jokes. I could see the lines on his face. He still looked foreign, I thought. But, for some reason, right then and there, as we drank our coffee, we both knew we were going to become lovers. We didn't have to say anything else.

We drove back to my loft. He walked all the dogs. Then we made love on the mattress, on the floor, in the late afternoon.

After we made love, we slept. When I awoke, it was past six. Patrice was dressed, sitting on the edge of the mattress, playing a game of fetch with Heineken and Stout that appeared to be getting out of hand. Bernstein strolled over to me to see if I was OK. I punched him ever so gently in the nose.

"I don't know how we got into this situation," I said.

"Opposites attract," he replied, "and besides," he added, "I told you I was in love with you. That's why I had to pull out all the stops."

"All the stops?"

"The Blue Whale. It always works. With out-of-work actresses, that is."

I laughed. For a real estate shark he was really a most delightful man. He seemed to enjoy poking fun at himself. Up close, he really was handsome in a sort of ascetic way. Like an aging, anorexic Jesuit. The lines on his face were pronounced. There was more white in his moustache and hair than I had realized. Oddly enough, when we were making love I had felt that I had known him a long time.

"I have to be going," he said.

"To harass a few tenants?" I asked.

"Something like that. Can I come back tonight with some food and wine?"

"Sure," I said.

He let himself out. After all, it was his building. He knew where the exits were.

For the next few hours I did absolutely nothing. I was waiting for him.

40

He came back about ten with a delicious Russian meal purchased from some exotic take-out place in the West Village which I had never heard of and a bottle of wine.

We ate a dozen small delicacies, the names of which I could hardly pronounce. Patrice threw the meat piroshkies to the dogs, who lined up for them as if they were at an athletic event.

After we had finished eating, I told Patrice about the dogs . . . where I had found each one . . . their peculiarities . . . their likes and dislikes. He listened as if he were listening to a financial proposition—politely, respectfully, asking intelligent questions that were somehow not really relevant.

Then he told me where he came from, what he was about, what he wanted. I wasn't really listening because they were delusions . . . about the city of tomorrow. He was a damned real estate shark and he loved me and somehow in some manner for some reason I had become involved with him—perhaps infatuated with him. I didn't want to fight. I would use him like he used me. We were lovers—that was its own reward. We were talking together—busting out of the incredible glacial isolation that this very dangerous city encased us in, perpetually.

Then we went to bed and made love and slept and woke up and made love again and slept. The dogs watched us, serenely scattered about the loft.

It was about 3:30 in the morning when I awoke again. Patrice lay beside me, sleeping softly. His naked body was lithe and strong and no longer young. He was that kind of middle-aged man who could function as one's father and one's son at the same time.

I stared past him toward the window—and froze. Someone was in the loft!

I was absolutely rigid with fear.

Then I realized what a fool I was. Patrice had hung his clothes on a chair and in the darkness they had seemed like a person.

I stared at the mirage. I couldn't take my eyes off his stupid clothes. The clothes were hung in such a way that the apparition seemed crucified—arms outstretched against the wood. Finally I turned away.

I closed my eyes. It wasn't an apparition. It was the ghost of Charlie Seven. It was a visitation. He was saying to me: Take who you want as a lover, even a landlord . . . but don't let me vanish . . . don't let it be forgotten . . . don't let it pass by.

But there was nothing I could do. Who was I? The NYPD? What power did I exercise? I was burdening myself with something I was not equipped to deal with. Wasn't it true that all I could do for Charlie Seven was mourn him?

I couldn't get back to sleep. Something else was gnawing at the back of my head. A name. A thing. A fact.

The dogs knew I was up, but they didn't approach. Patrice started to toss and turn and talk in his sleep.

Then it came to me. A possibility. If I could get some money I could get Digger.

Patrice would lend me money. Patrice's money would give me the power to hire Digger. And Digger, if I could find him, could help me put to rest the ghost of Charlie Seven.

Digger was a thief. A malnourished Hell's Kitchen thief. He was in his early twenties, tall, stooped, with a perpetually blemished skin. He had lived his whole life in a twenty-block radius, except for visits to upstate penitentiaries. He moved from apartment to apartment. He lived on sickeningly sweet cupcakes and spaghetti and meatballs in cans. He dressed like a patchwork quilt—part hoodlum, part biker, part dandy.

And I hadn't seen him in almost two years.

But he had helped me once. I had bought his help because that was the only way Digger operated. And he had delivered.

How to find him? Always a problem. The thief as will-o' the wisp.

The next morning, after Patrice left, and after I had walked the dogs, I wandered over to the Tenth Avenue grocery store where Digger used to hang out.

No one there had seen him lately. One old Hispanic man told me he thought Digger now hung out on Ninth Avenue around 46th Street.

So, for the next five hours, I walked back and forth from candy store to bodega, but Digger did not materialize.

In fact, it was he who found me. When I got back to my loft, he was standing in front of the building, blowing into his freezing hands.

"Looking for me?" he asked, in the same infuriatingly arrogant voice, touched with sexual innuendo, that he used with all women.

He looked worse than ever—pale, agitated, his face breaking out all over. He was wearing a crazy hat and was dressed for a spring day. He still had that funny West Side accent where the words sort of get choked to death before they come out.

When we got upstairs it was obvious that the dogs remembered him.

Even Molson bumped into him gently, as if he were a tall dog bone.

"I thought by now you'd be up in lights on Broadway. Sally Tepper starring in . . ." He paused, trying to think of a name of a hit show, then giving it up.

"No change," I said.

"Nice place, though."

"Just got it. I was evicted from my old apartment."

"Got any milk?" he asked.

"In the refrigerator."

He retrieved the container and drank from it.

"Who you sleeping with lately?" he asked, grinning and staring at the mattress.

"None of your business."

He drank more of the milk.

"What have you been doing lately, Digger?"

"Show biz," he said.

"Seriously."

"A little here, a little there."

"Where are you living?"

"One night here, one night there. What is this? A TV interview? Are you from 'Eyewitness News'? "

"I need your help, Digger."

"For what?"

"Remember Charlie Seven?"

"No."

"The tall wino with the beard who lived on the tracks?"

"No."

"He was murdered in the subway the other day."

"Shit happens," he noted, cynically.

"He was my friend, Digger."

"Well, some like winos; some like junkies."

"He wasn't the only derelict murdered recently."

"So I heard."

"I want you to make a list for me."

"What kind of list?"

"I want you to make a list of all the homeless people murdered in the past six months."

"Why?"

"I don't really know."

"Is that all?"

"No, I want you to find Charlie Seven's family."

"I thought you said he was homeless."

"It's not his real family. I'm talking about the people he lived with on the tracks—an old lady named Mrs. Toast, Sleepy, and Arthur. Another one of his family, a cripple, was also murdered."

"You want me to do all this for love?" he asked wickedly, pointing at the mattress.

"Five thousand dollars," I said.

"Man, that's a lot of curiosity."

"You can take a long rest from being a thief."

He stood still, fingering his hat.

"Yes or no, Digger."

"When do I get the bread?"

"When I get it."

"Which is when?"

"In a few days. I'll give you twenty-five hundred up front. Twelve-fifty when you bring me the list . . . twelve-fifty when you find Charlie's family."

It was funny the way I was apportioning the money, since I hadn't obtained it yet and didn't even know if Patrice would do it. I realized right then I could have gotten Digger for much less and had probably decided on the $5,000 figure because I knew Patrice had money.

"Done," Digger said.

"Where can I reach you?" I asked.

"You can't. I'll stop by in five days."

And then he was gone, leaving the now empty milk container on the floor.

8

So the landlord and I became an item, as they say. We were, in truth, more than just an item. There was him and there was the rest of my life. It was the kind of adolescent affair that only women in their mid-thirties experience; another desperate grasp at turning sexual infatuation into the promise of love.

I waited just a week before asking him to borrow the five thousand dollars.

Digger showed up in five days as promised and I told him to come back in five more. He arched his eyebrows. "Trust me, Digger," I said. He slunk off.

I asked Patrice for the money. Easily, and point blank, as we sat in a bar in the Hilton at about four o'clock in the afternoon, after we had made love in the loft. This bar had very comfortable divans, ideal for lovers. He was excited and talkative as I'd noticed he was, after sex. He was discoursing on hotel bars in general. We were both sipping ales.

I was playing with one of the beautifully embossed paper napkins that were scattered on the small glass table in front of the divan. It occurred to me, for no reason whatsoever, that one of the most profound differences between the haves and the have-nots was access to beautifully embossed paper napkins. What would Charlie Seven have thought about such a napkin? What would he have done with it?

Then I asked the question, right in the middle of his conversation, or rather, monologue.

I could feel his body tense ever so slightly and that made me feel good. It made me feel a bit wicked . . . that I was sleeping with a landlord whose only true rationale for existence was the bottom line. Why shouldn't giving out money agitate him slightly?

"You need five thousand dollars?"

"I need it fast."

"Why is it," he asked, kissing me gently on the side of the head, "that when people need money, they always need it fast?"

"Because money is energy."

"I thought actresses were more Freudian—I thought they believed that money is feces."

"Only when working. I'm an out-of-work actress."

"Why five thousand?"

"You want to lend me more?"

"I want to give you what you need."

"Not give, Patrice, *lend*. This is a loan. Not a gift."

"What do you need?"

"Five thousand."

"Will you take a check?" he asked.

"Do you have it in cash?"

"Not on me."

"A check is fine."

He pulled out his wallet and extracted a loose check, folded. He unfolded the check on the glass table and asked the waitress for a pen. He started to write. I leaned over with him. I found it, for some reason, to be a very intimate transaction: the whole business of him extracting the check, unfolding it, writing my name—all of it was intimate, erotic, as if we had moved into a different speed. He handed me the check. I inspected it carefully.

"You write funny," I said.

"You live funny," he replied.

"But you want to be with me?"

"Very much so."

"Why?"

"Because you're beautiful and angry and smart and difficult and—"

"And comparatively young."

"Yes. Very, very young. So young that you have no idea what to do."

"And you have an idea?"

"I'm a real estate developer. I have a lot of ideas."

"All of them bad."

"So you say."

"Are we going to fight?"

"I hope not."

"Good," I said and pressed his hand. I didn't want to argue with him then.

His face clouded over. He gestured almost imperceptibly with his head and the waitress walked over.

"A brandy," he said to her. "Remy, straight up," and to me he said, "To celebrate."

"What?"

"What's going on," he replied.

The way he had effortlessly got the waitress's attention irritated me. It was the gesture of a man who was used to underlings. He knew how to be served. Always. But that was not the real irritant. It was his unconscious assumption, always there, that this was *his* city. He was primary.

He could order things; command attention with a gesture. It was *his* city because he had bought chunks of it . . . destroyed chunks of it—built chunks of it. I could live a thousand years and never have that assurance. When I said New York was *my* city, it was a romantic notion, an impulse. Patrice meant it—on the most basic level.

Digger came again, in a few days, underdressed as usual, aggressive in his walk. His whole demeanor said: "Pay up."

I had deposited Patrice's $5,000 check in my account and then, after it had cleared, cashed my own check for $2,500 the next day. The teller asked me how I wanted it. I said in hundreds, thinking that Digger would like that denomination. And I was right.

He stood by a dimly lit window in my loft and counted out the bills—twenty-five of them—one by one, flicking them professionally.

When he had finished, he said: "Well, time to go to work."

"I think so."

"Do you really want a list?"

"Yes."

"I don't get what kind of list you want. You mean I should write it out?"

"Exactly. On a piece of paper, Digger. You remember how to write, don't you?"

"But what should I put on that list?"

It was a good question. I scratched one of Molson's large ears and he groaned. What kind of information did I want? I wanted facts that would confirm or deny an epidemic of death among the homeless. I wanted, even more, something that would illuminate the death of Charlie Seven.

"Here's what I want, Digger. The name of the person murdered, if available. Age and sex and color. How he or she was murdered. Where he or she was murdered. Whether or not anyone has been arrested for the crime."

"What about shoe size?" Digger interjected, sardonically.

"Twenty-five hundred should bring me a good list. It's better than stealing typewriters, Digger. And there's another twelve-fifty for you when I get it . . . and another twelve-fifty when you find Charlie's family."

"First things first," he said.

"Right. And the list is first."

He grinned at me and then very ceremoniously opened and began to chew a Reese's Peanut Butter Cup— his current main food source.

When he had finished he said: "Always trying to put the city right, huh? Don't you people ever learn?"

"What's to learn?"

"It can't be put right. Too much shit in the game."

He was street philosophizing, as usual.

"Just make that list, Digger."

"Count on it," he said, and was gone.

His visit exhausted me. I went right to sleep after he left and didn't get up until midnight when it was way past time to walk the dogs. They were prowling the apartment in an agitated state.

The first shift went fine.

On the second shift, consisting of Molson and Heineken, I had barely reached the corner of Eleventh Avenue when the ear-splitting sounds of fire engines exploded around us. Lights, horns, shouts. I pulled the dogs closer.

An abandoned building was smoking in the freezing night. Tiny darts of flames were visible through the haze.

For a moment I had the kind of hopelessness that comes when one feels one's entire habitat is crumbling . . . that things are simply falling away. And with that hopelessness comes fear. I couldn't move.

The firemen began their ritual. Lines of men moving into the building, carrying strange things on their shoulders.

The grinding of gears as machines began to perform

and then the gushing spirals of water spitting out trails of ice as they reached out for the fire and smoke.

I had seen this sight a dozen times in the past few weeks and this same paralyzing fear was always present.

But on this particular night it only lasted for seconds. Indeed, I actually pulled the dogs closer to the fire. I actually began to really watch.

After all, I was beginning to act, and not in the theatrical sense. I had obtained Digger's services. I would find out about Charlie Seven's death. I would find out about other deaths. I would find Charlie's missing family. I was once again more than just a pathetic conscience in a neighborhood that had lost its way—I was a force.

My new strength had overcome my old fears.

Watching, holding the dogs close, I also began to realize that this new strength, my new purpose, might well have stemmed from Patrice . . . from the fact that I had a lover . . . from the fact that he had provided an outlet, a goal, a pathway for passion.

I hesitated to use or even consider that old-fashioned word, "liberation." How could a landlord help me achieve that? But it was possible. Very, very possible.

9

"Sally, it's Beth. I'm a few blocks away. Can I stop over?"

Her voice was almost pleading over the phone. "Sure," I said.

It was an awkward time for her to visit. Patrice was picking me up shortly. It was going to be, believe it or not, our first formal old-fashioned "date." He was taking me for cocktails, then to a Madison Avenue art gallery for a preview, and then to a party on the Upper East Side. I was in the midst of dressing, about to put on a very formal and very elegant black dress, which I hadn't worn in eight years, with shoes and bag to match.

I finished dressing by the time Beth arrived. She stood in the loft without removing her hat and just stared at me in my finery, making strange clucking sounds.

I realized that in all the years I had known Beth White, she had never seen me dressed up.

I felt distinctly uncomfortable under her gaze.

"What are you doing?"

"Going to a party."

"I just came from the office. Someone saw Sleepy, one of Charlie Seven's family, about three days ago on the Lower East Side, around Houston Street. But that's all we could find out."

I was about to respond by telling her I had Digger looking for him and the others—but for some reason I decided against telling her. I just nodded in appreciation for the information.

"Whose party?" she then asked, switching conversational gears again, her face florid from the cold.

"Just a party."

"You mean a party in your new friend's world."

I didn't answer.

"Everybody knows what's going on with you and Stephen Patrice," she said.

"Look, Beth. I'm not a nun or an ex-nun. I never took any vows of chastity. In fact, I don't really believe in chastity. It's sort of like influenza."

"I'm not talking about chastity. I'm talking about common sense. How could you get into bed, rationally, with a man who uses this neighborhood to harvest the only crop he understands—cash?"

Budweiser had ambled over and stared up at the large woman. Beth bent over and patted her head, reluctantly. Her anger was evident.

There was nothing I could say to Beth. I couldn't even explain Stephen Patrice to myself. And the idea of going to a posh party with him both nauseated and intrigued me—as did my careful dressing. It was out of character. Maybe that was its charm .... like landing a role no one in a million years would ever have predicted for me.

"Do you want some coffee, Beth?"

"No, I don't want you to get any stains on your pretty, pretty dress."

"Beth, it's an affair, just an affair. Many people, you know, have them. Relax."

"Tell it to Charlie Seven," she replied, bitterly.

"What do you mean by that? Charlie Seven is dead."

"I mean that people like Patrice create poor souls, and destroy them."

"You're talking crazy, Beth."

"People like Patrice never go near a gun in their lives, but in their heart and soul, they're murderers."

"I thought you were a proponent of Christian love."

She started to answer and then didn't. For the first time since I had known Beth White, she appeared to be losing control. The indomitable Joan of Arc for the down-trodden seemed to be about to collapse because I was sleeping with a man. It was crazy, and it was crazier still that she seemed on the verge of tears.

Finally, she whispered, "I don't know too much about Christian love any more."

"Sit down, Beth," I said, and pulled over a chair for her. She sat, crumpled, as if she were suddenly exhausted beyond reason.

I busied myself with finishing the refashioning of Sally Tepper, forgetting the passage of time.

There was a knock on the door. It had to be Patrice. It was Patrice. I cursed inwardly. I didn't want him and Beth White to meet now, not given the way she was feeling.

But Beth was perfectly polite, though distant.

"I've heard of you," Patrice said, smiling, as he was introduced.

"And I've heard of you," Beth replied.

Two minutes later she was gone.

It was a very strange evening. The party with Patrice was memorable for me. The people there were probably a random cross-section of the city's elite—politically, culturally, and financially. I realized, after I had been at the party only a few minutes, that I was watching them as if they were a collection of exotic birds. I listened to their conversation as if they were talking a different and thoroughly nonsensical language. I drank the wine and ate the food as if it had been prepared by people from a different planet. And I watched Patrice move from cluster to cluster, easily, listening, smiling, chatting.

Only once during the party did some conversation truly nauseate me, and then, in a quiet fury, I poured some champagne slowly and deliberately on my lover's shoes. He smiled.

The taxi ride back to my loft was truly memorable because of a very funny chance event—though it did not seem funny to me at the time.

The cab was going west on 59th Street. It stopped for a light at Sixth Avenue. I leaned forward and stared out the window, looking downtown on Sixth.

There was a reason I looked out the window at that specific time. In the last few years Sixth Avenue between 57th and 59th streets had become a very kooky bordello—there were high-priced, good-looking white hookers on the corners and in the doorways.

The action intrigued me. I have never been one of those people who love hookers out of some perverse and sentimental romanticism. I pitied them and despised them. But these new Sixth Avenue hookers were a bit different—mainly because of their dress. It was like watching a very sophisticated vaudeville. One week the hookers would be dressed like businesswomen, right down to the ties. The next week they would all switch to girl's clothes, like checked skirts and parochial school blazers. Who called the fashion turns? Their pimps? And why?

When I looked out the cab window I saw what I was looking for—streetwalkers, dressed this time as Connecticut housewives, with cashmere sweaters.

But I also saw something I wasn't looking for—my friend Digger engaged in an earnest negotiation with one of them for their services. And he was wearing a brand-new lined denim jacket. So that was where the money was going.

It was astonishing. It was infuriating. I had given him a lot of money for a specific task and look what he was doing with it—whoring and buying clothes.

I turned to Patrice and was about to complain bitterly. Then I realized that it was Patrice who had given me the money and I had never told him what it was for. The whole thing was too absurd. I shut my mouth.

The cab pulled off. I calmed down. What did it matter what Digger did, as long as he got me the information I needed?

As the days passed, I settled into a groove. I started going to acting class again. I landed two or three temporary cashiering jobs—a day here, a day there.

Patrice and I saw each other about three days a week and he stayed over at least once a week. My loft was slowly being furnished. The dogs loved the place. Each one found his or her own private spot and they shared the common space with mock fights.

I was beginning to feel good about myself, not least because I was doing something about Charlie Seven. I was doing something about the world. Every time the phone rang I expected it to be Digger. Every time I saw someone walking down my street I thought it was Digger. When he finally did call it was only to say "It's coming."

So I waited. That Charlie Seven and Little Arthur were dead, and the rest of the family had vanished, meant nothing to Hell's Kitchen. Life went on without any memorials whatsoever. Abandoned buildings burned. Homeless people froze to death. The Broadway theaters boomed. The addicts scored. The pious prayed. And those caught in the middle, raising children and going to work, just got more perplexed and more impotent.

Digger called for real on a cold morning during the

56

second week of February. I had just finished the elaborate feeding ritual with the dogs: positioning the bowls at least three feet from each other . . . giving each one special snacks . . . requisite vitamins . . . cautioning each of them to stick to his or her own feeding bowl and avoid confrontations.

I placed the bowls and the mayhem started. I retired to my mattress and watched, hoping, as usual, that it would not get out of hand.

Then the phone rang and Digger said: "You owe me twelve-fifty." So I knew he had done it. I told him it would take me a few days to get him the rest of the money, but I needed the information now.

He was at the loft in fifteen minutes, grinning from ear to ear.

I had recently purchased a large beat-up old oak table with four straw-backed chairs and Digger went straight to that table and began, to my astonishment, to empty his pockets on it.

He kept pulling out scraps of paper—all sizes and shapes.

"Here's your list," he said triumphantly.

I stared down at the scraps. "What is this, Digger?"

"What you asked for."

I sat down and began to smooth out the crumpled pieces. Finally I understood. Digger's idea of a list was to put one individual on one piece of paper.

"Twenty-nine," Digger said.

"Twenty-nine what?"

"Twenty-nine murders," he replied, grinning.

Suddenly, Stout, having finished his food, streaked across the room, snatched up one of the loose pieces of paper from the edge of the table and flew back to his bowl. "Bad dog!" I screamed at him, and it took me five minutes to corner him and catch him and retrieve the now sodden half-chewed slip.

Then I carefully gathered the pieces of paper—some obviously cut-up wrapping paper—and stacked them.

I began to read. Yes, Digger had done his job.

On each piece of paper was a name. Sometimes it was just a nickname, but it was a name or the word "Unidentified" or "Noname." And after the name or noname came the sex, approximate age, race, place of his or her death, date, and how murdered.

I sat there for a long time, shuffling the pieces of paper. It was hard for me to realize that all these pieces of paper represented murdered humans.

I looked at Digger.

"What the hell's the matter?" he demanded. "That's what you wanted, isn't it?"

I nodded. I began to read each slip carefully, Digger hovering by my side to translate when his writing was indecipherable.

It was a journey through a special kind of hell. Some had been stabbed to death ... some hung ... some torched ... some shot ... some beaten to death. Some had died on the street ... some in the subway ... some in doorways. Some had died in Manhattan ... some in the Bronx ... some in Brooklyn ... some in Queens and Staten Island.

The only connection was no connection at all: they were all homeless, all derelict, all murdered.

After the initial shock of those pieces of paper had faded, I tried to understand what they signified.

Twenty-nine homeless people murdered in a six-month period. But did that indicate an epidemic? Was there a conspiracy? Or was it only the way of this particular world?

I mean, in Hell's Kitchen, during any given week in the winter, probably ten homeless people end up as corpses from the cold, from fights, from accidents.

"So what does it mean?" Digger asked.

"I don't know."

"It wasn't easy getting all this. I had to dig. I asked cops. I asked hustlers and psychos. I asked anyone. Sure, some of the stuff was in old newspapers. But most wasn't. You know who helped me the most? For a price? Security guards in the hospital emergency wards. That I figured out myself—that they would know. And they did."

"You did well, Digger. I'll get you the next payment soon."

"And now I'll find those crazies for you."

"What crazies?"

"That dead wino's family."

I made us both a cup of coffee and some toast. Digger gobbled the toast after smearing half a bottle of raspberry jam over the slices.

The slips of paper were between us on the table. How arrogant I had been! I was going to justify Charlie Seven's horrible death. I was going to investigate, act, pay back. That's what I thought I was going to do. The delusions of an out-of-work actress! All I had were pieces of paper—random death notices.

Gool old impressionable Sally Tepper, still playing the wrong part on the wrong stage. A friend of mine had been murdered. A transit cop had tried to impress me with his coolness and his cynicism by spinning a tale of unreported mass murder. A few homeless people had moved on. And I had developed a full-blown conspiracy theory; I had borrowed money and hired a thief.

"You like my new jacket?" Digger the thief asked. I nodded in assent, not telling him that I had seen it on him before, on 57th Street, when he was propositioning a hooker.

I stared at the pile of slips again. I realized what was happening; I was beginning to feel sorry for myself; I was beginning to make fun of myself—to characterize all my thoughts as delusions.

I was giving up before I started. Digger had given me a treasure chest of death. It was up to me to deal with it.

"Let's go over them again, Digger."

"Why not?"

"Can you read them out loud?"

"Sure, but why?"

"A connection, Digger, I'm looking for a connection between them."

"They're all dead," he said.

"Besides that, about the way they died, maybe—or why."

Digger picked up the slips and read them one by one. I listened. It was hard to concentrate. I closed my eyes. When he finished the last one, I opened them.

"I don't get any connection," Digger said, "except maybe that those who got ice-picked have something in common—and those who got torched—you know what I mean . . . the M.O."

"I asked you to find out if any suspects had been arrested."

"That was hard. I couldn't do it. Remember . . . I didn't get most of this stuff from the cops."

"How did you really get it, Digger?"

"I told you. A little here, a little there. But most of it from emergency wards in hospitals."

"Which ones?"

"Well, I picked the two busiest emergency wards in each of the five boroughs. Manhattan, Bronx, Brooklyn, Queens, Staten Island. Hell, that's why I couldn't get names on all of them."

For the first time I realized there was a peculiarity in the list. I shuffled through the slips quickly to confirm it. Yes, I had been right. There was only one slip for a Staten Island murder and only two for Queens.

I mentioned the peculiarity to Digger. He shrugged. It meant nothing to him.

60

I went through the list again, looking for a borough count. Nine of the murders were in Manhattan. Nine were in the Bronx. Eight were in Brooklyn.

Then I placed them into separate borough piles.

"Why are you doing that?" Digger asked.

"I don't know, Digger. But something is strange about where they were killed."

"What do you mean, 'strange'?"

"It's a geographic pattern," I noted.

"Where?"

I left the table, went to the kitchen cabinet where I kept a yellow legal pad, and returned with a loose sheet of paper. I was excited now, anticipatory. The geographic logic of the slips was unfolding.

"Look, Digger," I said, drawing a very crude map of New York City.

"I'm looking. So what?"

"Read me each slip again."

"Why?"

"Just do it."

As he read each slip I made a cross at approximately where each had been murdered.

When he was finished, I drew a line through the crosses.

"Look again, Digger," I said.

He stared at my crude marked map.

The line, with a few exceptions, went from the tip of the Bronx south through Manhattan and then through Brooklyn, ending near Coney Island.

"Weird," he whispered.

"Very weird, Digger. All these murders seem relentlessly to wind through Bronx, Manhattan, and Brooklyn on a more or less north-south line and then turn southeast to the ocean. It's too weird to be chance."

"Yeah, but what does it mean?"

"I don't know yet. But I'll find out."

Digger lit a cigarette. "You know," he said, "for an actress, you're one smart lady."

"Help me walk the dogs, Digger."

"That's not what I'm being paid for."

"Well, you're not being paid to make it with high-price streetwalkers on Sixth Avenue, either."

His eyes narrowed; then he laughed. He helped me walk the dogs.

10

I was in my bed with Patrice. It was about two o'clock in the morning. We were both staring out the windows, where a light snow was falling. Bernstein and Heineken, for some reason, were prowling about the loft, alternately growling and whining. I think they were after a mouse. The other dogs were either snoring or dreaming.

Patrice touched my foot with his.

"This is the first time we made love and you were disinterested."

"It happens," I replied.

He laughed and asked: "Did I do something wrong?"

"No. As I said, it happens."

"Nothing just happens with you, Sally."

"Is that a compliment?"

"I don't know. It's just a fact."

"I have things on my mind," I said.

Patrice had been getting a bit difficult lately. He wanted me to affirm him and the affair. He wanted me to reciprocate his love. That I couldn't do. I did still want the affair to continue. I felt his closeness to be important—physically, emotionally, and, oddly enough, spiritually. At the most banal level, he made me feel good. At the most sublime level, he somehow gave me the courage to act.

And I relished the fact that some kind of intimacy with another human being had been established. It gave me a sense of health, of normalcy. But I couldn't make that intimacy apparent with him. Something was missing in everything but our lovemaking. He wanted to talk with me, share with me. He wanted to merge.

"What kind of things, Sally?"

"They wouldn't interest you."

"Try me."

"Go to sleep, Patrice."

He kissed me and turned away. I lay there without moving. The snowflakes seemed to have grown larger.

What was on my mind was what I had discovered from those stupid little slips of paper. I knew that the strange pattern—the north to southeast line across the map—meant something important. But what? Why that pattern of death? It was too bizarre to be random.

I waited until Patrice had fallen asleep and then went to the table where the slips and the map lay.

I flicked on the first bulb of a three-bulb lamp. Molson groaned, stood, and then ambled over to investigate. He was disappointed and collapsed at the foot of the table.

I stared at the pattern of death I had superimposed over my map of the city.

It was absurd, I realized, but no matter how many times I stared at it, it looked as if it had been constructed by a bunch of madmen who had murdered derelicts in a row, from north to south.

It was as if they had planted trees on a road. No, it was as if they had crucified them on the road to Rome—

like the survivors of Spartacus's slave revolt had been crucified on the Appian Way.

The word "road" intrigued me. It *was* a road. I knew
that. But what kind? What was I talking about?

Worse, the longer I looked at the crude map, the more
I felt that I knew the road . . . I knew the pattern. Like a
road that one uses to go to school or to work. Like a familiar
path in the woods.

But this one was across a city. I had never walked or
driven from the Bronx to Coney Island.

But I had ridden. The map seemed to dance in my
hand. Yes, I had ridden that path . . . *underground.*

I stared at the map. I knew what I was looking at: a
map of the "D" train.

They had been murdered along the route of the "D"
train . . . from 205th Street in the Bronx to Coney Island
in Brooklyn.

That's why there were so few dead in Queens and
Staten Island. The "D" train doesn't go there.

It was crazy. But there it was.

I went back to bed. Patrice was sleeping. I woke him
up. He looked at me, dazed. I was high as a kite . . . excited . . . totally enthralled by my own deductive powers. I
didn't want to tell him what I was doing, what I had discovered, but I wanted to share with him in some way my
triumph. So I kissed him out of his daze and we made
love.

He left much later than usual in the morning, at about
eight, misinterpreting my passion of the night before.

I had a lot of things to do and not much time to do
them. I went to the bank to get Digger's money. I went to
the cleaner to take out a dress I was wearing for a lunchtime
cashiering job—from eleven to three. I walked and fed
the dogs.

Digger showed up around ten, trying to be casual.

I was still high from the night before . . . almost
manic . . . juggling seven tasks and concepts at the same

65

time. It frightened Digger a bit; thieves don't like irrational people.

"I have the money, Digger, but I don't want to give it to you here."

"Why not?"

"I like variety. I gave you the first payment here. I want to give you the second payment somewhere else."

"It's your money," he shrugged, "but it's stupid."

"Humor me, Digger, humor me."

"Sure," he assented.

I gathered my bag, my pencil, my social security card, and whatever else I needed for the cashiering job and walked out, Digger following.

"Where are we going?" he asked.

"Fifty-seventh and Seventh."

He cursed under his breath and we headed uptown into the freezing wind.

When we reached the corner of Fifty-seventh Street and Seventh Avenue I started down into the subway.

"Wait a minute. Where the hell are we going?"

"Just humor me, Digger," I repeated. I went to the token booth, purchased two tokens, and asked for a subway map. I put one token in the machine for me and another for him, and slid through.

"I don't want no subway ride," Digger said.

"No ride. Just a peek," I explained.

He went through. I walked down to the platform and waited. He waited with me.

"What are we doing here?" he asked, angry, confused.

"This is where I pay you, Digger," I said, and handed him the envelope that contained $1,250. He opened the envelope quickly, closed it quickly, and stuffed it into his new jacket, buttoning the pocket.

He started to walk away.

"Wait, Digger, wait."

We could sense the rumble. A train was approaching

the station. It broke out of the tunnel with a whoosh and screamed down on us. Then, with a diminishing whooshing and hissing it braked to a halt and the doors flew open.

"Look, Digger," I said, pointing at the side of the train.

"I'm looking. So what? It's a 'D' train."

The doors remained open.

"You know the stops on the 'D' train?"

"Some of them."

I opened the map and read them to Digger: "Fifty-seventh and Seventh, Forty-second and Broadway, Thirty-fourth and Broadway, Fourteenth and Broadway, Canal and Broadway, then, in Brooklyn—Dekalb, Atlantic, Seventh . . ."

Digger stopped me: "I know, I know, on to Coney Island."

"What about the other 'D' train, Digger?"

"What is this? A goddamn transit authority quiz? The other 'D' train goes to the Bronx."

"Right, Digger. The split service in the 'D' train sends the other one along Sixth Avenue rather than Broadway, from 34th and Sixth, to 42nd and Sixth, 53rd and Seventh, Columbus Circle, 125th Street, and on up to 205th Street and Bainbridge Avenue in the Bronx."

I stopped and stared at him. He didn't understand the connection I was making.

I walked up the stairs and out of the station. It was getting late. I had to be at the job a little after eleven. The restaurant was on Fifty-sixth and Ninth.

"What do you want me to do next? Stare at the 'F' train?" Digger asked sardonically.

I started to walk toward the restaurant. Digger followed.

"Why don't you just say what you want to say instead of all this actress bullshit?"

"The slips, Digger, remember the slips. You wrote them out."

67

"I remember them."

"The stops on the 'D,' Digger. The stops and the slips . . . the slips and the stops . . ."

He stared at me. He was making the astonishing connection.

"Get it, Digger? Most of the murders happened at specific stops of the 'D' . . . either in the stations or close by, on the street."

"That's crazy. That's the craziest thing I ever heard."

We started walking again.

"It's spooky," Digger added.

We kept walking. We came to the restaurant. I was astonished. The Garden, as it was called, was a Chinese restaurant! I had never cashiered in a Chinese restaurant in my life. I had never seen a Caucasian cashier in a Chinese restaurant, or, for that matter, a Caucasian waiter.

I looked at Digger. He had become agitated, unable to light a cigarette in the wind.

"The whole thing is crazy. Why would anyone murder people, winos, along the 'D' train line. It can't be, Sally. I mean, I know it is, but it don't mean a goddamn thing." He was talking quickly and quietly now. I could barely hear him.

"You mean it's a coincidence?"

"Why not?"

"Too many, Digger, too many."

"If you're wrong, we're idiots, Sally. And if you're right. So what? It's like reporting a theft in the joint. What the hell does it mean? You gonna go to the cops? They'll laugh you out. What do you have? Nothing. A goddamn subway map and a lot of long gone corpses—none with mailing addresses—and all buried already or burned or whatever the hell they do to winos."

"I don't know what I'm going to do."

Digger made a gesture with his hand, of futility, of contempt, and perhaps of hatred of me that I had got him involved in this thing, in spite of the money.

I walked into the restaurant. It was one of those new wave Chinese restaurants without MSG. Small, very neat tables with absolutely white tablecloths. Dark walls. Quiet, very quiet. Glistening tile floors. Small, artful portions, no doubt. To my astonishment, they had an old-fashioned cash register. I hadn't worked one of them in years; nowadays, the restaurants use the computer models. The waitress just codes it and the computer does the rest—itemizing, pricing, totaling, figuring tax, everything.

An aged Chinese man wearing a blue suit greeted me warmly. When I told him that I had forgotten how to work the old register, he patiently showed me, explaining that their usual model was out for repair.

Then I settled into the high chair by the window and just waited. It was obvious that the only reason I had been hired for the day was that someone was sick—indeed, the entire restaurant seemed short-handed.

The luncheon trade started to trickle in. Most of them were out-of-towners on their way to a show or movie or shopping.

A few of them, in fact, looked like the Henri Bendel crowd who had inadvertently wandered too far west—way too far. The owner, or manager, asked me to help with the seating as the people came in. I did my best, a bit angry that he was paying me for only one task and asking me to double as a hostess. A few of the patrons were absolutely astonished at being greeted by a statuesque red-headed Caucasian.

About the only enjoyable aspect of the job was that I dealt with customers at the end of the meal. In restaurants with the computer registers, the check is paid at the table. The waitress is the only one I see. But with the old type cash register, the patron brings the check up to the register just prior to leaving. So there I was, like when I first started cashiering, taking the check, smiling, making change. It was almost, one might say, charming.

At around 2:15 the restaurant began to empty. My

69

fingers hurt from punching the keys. The tempo slowed down. I could see the kitchen help staring out at me through the window in the swinging door.

Two of the Henri Bendel set finished their lunch and came to the register. One of them, a short, thin woman wearing a fur coat and one of those dazzling high-neck cashmere dresses with a pearl choker, missed the handoff, and the check fluttered away between us.

I reached out for it. She did also. I missed it. She caught it. We both laughed.

Then she stared at me and said: "My God, you're Sally Tepper."

I admitted that was my name and looked at her, perplexed. I didn't know the woman from Adam.

"God, have I changed that much, Sally? It's me. Janet Heisler."

I was absolutely stunned. It must have been about ten years. We had been in the same acting class for a long time. But then she had given acting up, as many do, disgusted at her inability to land a role, hating the poverty and the hustles, hating the entire milieu.

She started to talk like a machine gun; about her husband and her kids and her activities and her house in a place called Wilton, Connecticut. She told me how she always spoke about Sally Tepper to her husband and friends, about how she saw me in one of my last parts—a small off-Broadway role three years ago—but just felt funny going backstage, about how she was so happy I was still hanging in there, about how I was so gifted sooner or later the parts would come.

Her friend was staring at me as if I were some kind of interesting mutant. Then Janet grabbed a napkin and began to write on it in large botched letters her address, her phone number, and, for all I knew, her social security number.

We embraced and she left, flustered, talking nervously at the top of her voice.

I was slipping into a deep depression when the manager beckoned me. His kindly face was in a snarl. There was a phone call for me. Didn't I know, his face said, that I wasn't supposed to get personal calls while working?

It was Digger. He said simply: "I found one of them. I found Mrs. Toast!"

I couldn't answer. I was stunned. I was happy.

He'd be at my loft, he said, about six, and he'd take me to her. Then he hung up.

11

Digger lay on the floor, his feet on one of the window ledges. My five dogs surrounded him, on their haunches—salivating, groaning, begging, threatening, howling—as Digger calmly peeled one slice of thinly sliced muenster cheese from the pound's worth he held in his hand. Then he placed it in a dog's mouth, being careful that his fingers weren't amputated in the lunge. Thus he went around the circle, giving cheese to each, trying to keep the dogs from attacking each other while waiting for their turn to come around again.

It was a madhouse and everyone was enjoying themselves immensely. When the last piece was consumed, Digger held out his empty hands and the dogs slunk off. God, how they loved cheese!

"It wasn't no brilliant bit of detective work, to tell the truth. After I left you at the restaurant I went to that Mexican place—that bar on Fifty-seventh and Tenth—and had some burritos and a couple of beers to try and digest all that 'D' train stuff. When I got out I figured that since I was close to the piers I'd go over and see if any of the big ships were berthed. Anyway, when I reached Fifty-seventh and Twelfth, I see a couple of derelicts huddled around a garbage can fire just near that Department of Sanitation garage. So I ask them about your friends . . . about Charlie Seven's friends. One of them says the lady named Mrs. Toast is just around the corner. So I go and see her and ask her if her name is Mrs. Toast, and she says yes."

"Did you think any more about the 'D' train, Digger?" I asked, changing the subject as I dressed warmly.

"No, no," he replied.

"Why not?"

"I can't handle two things at the same time."

"I've been thinking about it. And the more I think the more scary it becomes."

"You want me to take you to that old lady, or not?" Digger asked, growing impatient.

Off I went with him, the dogs groaning and whining at my departure as if they were dying of a collective broken heart—but I understood that it was Digger they mourned for and his thinly sliced muenster cheese.

As we headed toward Twelfth Avenue, I confided in Digger: "I think you were right about my not going to the cops. I think they wouldn't have any interest in it. I was thinking that we should go straight to the Justice Department . . . the way they used to do it in the South when they couldn't get a murder conviction because of lack of evidence . . . they would start a case about the victim's civil rights being violated."

"There," Digger said, pointing. We were in the middle of the block between Eleventh and Twelfth. He was pointing across the street toward the corner. I could make out a person in a doorway of a boarded-up store.

My eyes suddenly filled with tears and I began to

hurry. The reality of Mrs. Toast was like a happy ending; at least I knew that one of Charlie Seven's family was safe.

When we were about five feet away from her, we stopped, or rather, I stopped, and held Digger back with my hand.

There was something wrong. It was Mrs. Toast—but it wasn't Mrs. Toast.

She still had her shopping cart, but what was inside was piled neatly. Her grill was nowhere in sight. She was wearing the same kind of clothes, sweater upon sweater and ragged balloon pants, but her clothes seemed to lay peacefully upon her rather than in the usual disarray. Her face, which was usually contorted in some kind of rage or mirth or pain, was calm—and just watching the two of us as we approached.

"Mrs. Toast, do you remember me?"

She nodded her head thoughtfully. Digger and I moved close.

For the first time since I had known her, I realized that her hair was white.

"Where are your friends?" I asked.

"Oh, there are so many friends . . . so many lovely friends. And a garden with pots. Large pots."

She was still crazy, obviously. Her conversation was still absurd. But the delivery was decidedly different.

"Charlie is dead, Mrs. Toast, and Little Arthur. Where is Sleepy? Have you seen Sleepy? And Arthur? Have you seen him?"

I kept looking past her into the building shadows for a glimpse of Arthur and Sleepy. They had to be with her. They looked after her. They all looked after Mrs. Toast. Arthur used to push her cart sometimes. A thin, cadaverous man with a scraggly beard and moustache and a long filthy army overcoat without buttons, he would talk to Mrs. Toast incessantly, but she rarely answered. Arthur's conversation was often confusing to sane people, much less borderline psychotics like Mrs. Toast. And Sleepy was the

74

most protective of them all. A huge man with a dreadful skin condition on his face, he seemed to roll rather than walk through Hell's Kitchen. People used to call him the Jolly Green Giant.

She had to know where they were. I asked again: "Please, Mrs. Toast. Think. Where is Arthur? Where is Sleepy? When was the last time you saw them?"

She didn't answer my questions. She was gazing placidly at Digger, who was becoming distinctly uncomfortable under her gaze.

"Why did you leave the tracks?" I asked her.

She just smiled at me, and said: "Kennedy sent me a check this month. The poor man. All that money."

Digger whispered in my ear: "Look, I found her. You talked to her. She's OK. Now let's get out of here."

I motioned with my hand that we would go shortly.

"Where is your toast machine?" I asked.

"Do you want some toast, Dearie?" she asked.

She raised her hands as if to apologize for her lack. Something flashed before my eyes in the half darkness. I moved closer. Underneath her sweaters was a kind of white linen shirt with fringes.

I reached out and touched one of the fringes. She smiled. I remembered what the transit cop had said to me: about how, when they found Charlie Seven hanging, he was wearing a weird white shirt. I remembered that I had mocked the notion.

"What is this, Mrs. Toast?" I asked.

She stared down at the white shirt she was wearing, so obviously homemade, and pulled the sweaters higher with a kind of joyous defiance so that I could see the beginning of a design of a buffalo skull or something resembling it that had been woven or painted onto the fabric.

"No toast, Dearie," she whispered, and rearranged her clothes so that the strange white shirt was now hidden. A gust of wind blew suddenly and violently from the river, half spinning all three of us around.

That she now had one of those shirts was bizarre, if indeed it were the same as Charlie's. It confirmed what the transit cop had said. Obviously, she must have gotten it from Charlie or given it to Charlie. But why were they wearing such stupid garments? Where had they obtained them?

"Let's get out of here," Digger pleaded.

I said good-bye to Mrs. Toast. I cautioned her to go into a shelter if it got colder. I asked her to keep her eyes out for the rest of Charlie Seven's family, and if she found them to please tell Beth White at the League office.

Then Digger and I began to walk east. I was confused. And, for some reason, frightened.

"It's her . . . but it's not her. Do you know what I mean?" I asked Digger.

At the corner he stopped and said: "I know exactly what you mean."

And then he handed me a small object.

I moved under a streetlight.

"I found it ten feet away from her," he explained.

I was staring down at a used, disposable morphine syrette.

"It can't be hers," I said.

"Why not?"

"Where would she get the money for morphine?"

"I don't know. It's weird. These are the kind of syrettes army medics use when you get shot, to ease the pain."

It couldn't be. No one in Charlie Seven's family did drugs. Drugs were for those who were together enough to steal or hustle. The best they could do was a little cheap wine once in a while. But then again, it would explain her change. It would explain why she was so calm, why she was so focused. It would explain the new way she had looked at us—not with her usual fright or rage or perplexity.

We walked back to the doorway. Mrs. Toast was gone. We heard a sound beyond the building line. She had prob-

76

ably sought shelter deep inside the abandoned store. Digger lit a match with cupped hands. Three or four more used syrettes were scattered on the ground.

"We have to find out where she's getting this stuff," I said.

The white shirt. The morphine. The "D" train. Every step was getting more confusing and more threatening.

12

I was standing, huddled, in a doorway, on 56th Street between Eleventh and Twelfth Avenues. From where I stood, I could lean forward just a bit and see Mrs. Toast, who was standing in her doorway, half a block to the west. It was about 10:30 in the morning.

Digger and I had decided that it was crucial to discover the source of Mrs. Toast's morphine. We had decided on around-the-clock shifts of five hours each.

To ease the cold I walked in a small circle, like a psychotic toy soldier—stiff legs, stiff arms, swinging in unison. It made me a bit dizzy but it worked for the cold—it warmed me up.

The thought came to me that I was mimicking Charlie Seven's style of walking. But it was Charlie who had mimicked someone else. Anyway, it had been one of Charlie Seven's schizy modes of walking. He had many.

I peeked out. Mrs. Toast was still in place and alone.

I realized how much I missed Charlie Seven. He had been, in retrospect, like a grotesque ornament in my life. I felt a sense of shame. My concern for the homeless, for people like Charlie and his family, had never been pure . . . had never been truly authentic . . . had never been really based on love of my fellow creatures. It was something else—and I never understood it. The memory of Charlie Seven walking made me wince. I could not think about him anymore without thinking about the way they found him. And I could not think about his murder without thinking about the route of the "D" train and the other anonymous souls snuffed out.

What, I wondered, would Charlie Seven think of Mrs. Toast now, if he were alive? How would Charlie have reacted to a calm, almost reflective Mrs. Toast? Would Charlie know what morphine was?

I checked my watch. Only two hours left on my five-hour shift. A boat horn sound came from the river, like a frog in pain.

Mrs. Toast's back was to me. She was facing the river, maybe intrigued by the sound of the horn. I caught a flash of white. It was that stupid badly sewn shirt she was wearing . . . the one with the design, the one Charlie was supposed to have been wearing when he died.

I tried to think about it, but it made no sense. I tried to think about it as another pertinent fact, but it didn't fit anywhere. The clothing of the homeless never made sense.

Mrs. Toast vanished into the building. She came out in about fifteen minutes slowly eating what seemed to be a ragged chocolate bar.

It made me laugh for some reason—her eating that chocolate bar. The cold was going to my brain, making me giddy. Or perhaps it was the headiness of trying to construct a causal chain, of trying to relate everything to everything else, of trying to take each piece of information and tie it to the next piece—"D" train, white shirt, morphine, murder, on and on. Perhaps I realized I had become totally paranoid in Hell's Kitchen. For wasn't that the classical symptom of true paranoia: the belief that things that have no real connection with each other are really related, caused, interfered with by each other. It was the paranoia of the street. A woman yells three blocks away and the homeless paranoid derelict believes the cops are coming for him. Had I reached that level of lunacy? Had I created my own theater?

If Mrs. Toast could eat while under surveillance, I could eat while conducting that surveillance. So I pulled out an orange and peeled it inside my coat to keep my fingers from freezing.

After Mrs. Toast finished the chocolate, she began to eat what looked like an equally bedraggled piece of pastry, then half a banana, and then she drank some liquid out of a container. After dining, she took a walk and I followed her. But the walk was simply a very slow, almost stately circumnavigation of the block.

Finally, my tour was over and I passed the baton to Digger, who was grumbling a lot and complaining that the original contract had not stipulated surveillance for five *frozen* hours at a time on the goddamn street. My heart bled for him.

I went back to the loft and took care of the dogs. Patrice called and wanted to come over. I gave him a lame excuse. He was very sad. I made some hot cocoa, had a brief conversation with Budweiser, and then curled up on the mattress and read a few pages in a book I never could finish: a psychoanalytic study of female adolescence as depicted in a few novels like *The Prime of Miss Jean Brodie* by Muriel Spark . . . a book and a movie and a play I had always loved, particularly after someone told me I looked and moved like Maggie Smith, who played Miss Brodie in the movie.

Then I fell asleep, having set the alarm for the next shift. And so it went. Five hours on, five hours off, a kind of fast-moving perpetual blur.

It was on the fifth or maybe the sixth of Digger's shifts that something happened.

The phone woke me. I looked at the clock. It was two in the morning. Digger told me he was at a pay phone; he couldn't talk; I should get there fast.

I ran out of the loft, deciding not to take any of the dogs, and found Digger away from our surveillance building; closer to Mrs. Toast's building.

Digger pointed to the abandoned store, excited. "They're both inside. I saw the old lady get the syrettes. The pusher is in there with her."

"Did you ever see him in the neighborhood?"

"It's not a he. It's a woman," Digger said.

The street was deserted and empty. The elevated West Side Highway running over Twelfth Avenue cast a moonlit shadow down the center of the windblown street.

We waited. What were they doing inside?

"There," Digger said, pointing. I could see nothing.

"They're coming out. They're standing right by the building. Do you see their shadows?"

I didn't at first. Then they were in view. They seemed to be talking heatedly about something. Digger was right. It was a woman.

The stranger turned around and started to walk toward Eleventh Avenue.

"My God," I exclaimed, involuntarily, in a too loud whisper.

"Do you know her?"

"It's Beth White."

"Who the hell is Beth White?"

"Digger, you got it all wrong. She doesn't deal drugs. She's a friend of mine. She's one of the directors of the West Side League for the Homeless. She probably just came to make sure the old woman is OK."

"I don't care if she's the Deputy Mayor. I saw her hand the syrettes to the old lady. I saw her give the old lady the morphine." Digger was adamant.

I didn't know what to do. It was too much. It was too bizarre. Beth White? The number one holy roller do-gooder in Hell's Kitchen distributing morphine syrettes to the homeless?

She was near the corner and about to cross over.

"What do we do?" Digger asked.

He was always asking me those stupid questions.

"Follow her," I said.

So we followed her. The streets were absolutely deserted. It was too cold and too late for muggers or hookers or crazies.

She turned south on Ninth Avenue for a block, then went east on 55th.

We kept half a block behind, near the building line, her large bulky figure like a beacon in some lighthouse.

She turned south again on Seventh Avenue.

"She's going to the subway," Digger said.

And she surely was. Not an odd thing to do, usually—maybe she was going to visit an insomniac aunt at three in the morning—the trouble was she was walking down the steps to a "D" train stop—that goddamn "D" train.

We went down after her, slowly, carefully, not knowing where in the station she would be. She was standing at the center of the platform. We stayed just off the platform, behind the turnstiles, earning suspicious stares from the token booth clerk, buttressed in his fortress.

We waited. It seemed to be colder in the subway than out on the street. Beth was standing with her arms folded, staring down at the tracks. She looked as if she were deep in some philosophical problem.

"She's waiting for a train," Digger whispered, incredulously, his voice cracking from the cold, "she's waiting for a goddamn train." Then he added, astonished: "But what else would she be down here for?"

The train came in about twelve minutes. When it entered the station Digger and I deposited our tokens, walked through, and turned away from her. She saw nothing.

The doors opened. We waited. Beth didn't move.

"What the hell is she doing?"

I didn't know. The train pulled out. After it had vanished from the station, Beth walked toward the far end of the platform. Before our astonished eyes she climbed down the narrow steps and vanished into the pitch black tunnel.

We walked to the edge and peered into the darkness. I couldn't see a thing except for the faint glitter of the rails and, in the distance, a yellow signal.

"What is she doing?" Digger asked, panicky. "What the hell is that lunatic doing? You can't go into a subway tunnel like that. I don't care if she stashes a truckload of morphine down there. I ain't going after her. I ain't following that lady into the tunnel."

I was as frightened as he was. My idea of the subway was a hodgepodge of myths and fears and lurid old wives' tales. I believed there were cats down there as big as cougars, and alligators and snapping turtles and bats that sucked the blood from your eyes. I had old, half-remembered memories: of a kid who once chased a ball onto the third rail and had to be pulled off with a wooden stick, half roasted alive; of a crazy woman who decided she could fly and leaped from the top of the elevated tracks on 125th and Broadway to the sound of the wheels of the Broadway local. I had little snippets of old newspaper features—about trains that rolled through the subways late at night picking up the garbage, clanking, ferocious trains, like massive vacuum cleaners, about legendary transit authority employees who fixed the third rails with the current still on. I had visions of graffiti artists—*Taki 138*—and perverts in niches along the damp walls of the tunnels, hanging there like lizards. And loonies who pushed people off platforms because God commanded them to do so. All I had in my head were pieces of fact and fantasy garnered from many years of riding subways and thinking about them and running from them.

All I could say was: "Why would she keep morphine

down there? Digger, what is she doing in that tunnel?"

We stood at the edge of the platform, our feet playing with the small ladder that went down to the tracks but never setting foot on it.

I kept repeating over and over: "Digger, what is she doing in there? Why did she go into the tunnel?"

Digger shook me. Then he pulled me, pushed me, pulled me out of the station and into an all night grocery store.

We leaned against a freezer cabinet and sipped steaming hot coffee from containers. Digger ate two long, stale crullers which, from time to time, he dipped into his coffee.

We had become calm. We could think. We were safe. And, above all, we were warm.

"Digger, I think something terrible is happening. I think something is happening in the neighborhood . . . in the city . . . like some kind of creeping, crawling horror that first destroyed people like Charlie Seven and now is about to destroy Beth White and soon, whatever it is, will come for us . . . for all of us . . . for you and me and the dogs."

"All I saw was a fat lady going to get her morphine stash," he said, recovering his macho cynicism.

"But in a tunnel of the 'D' train. Remember, Digger, the 'D' train. Remember the slips. Remember the pattern I drew for you on the map."

I was beginning to think clearly again. It was necessary to go down there, at the least, to find out what poor Beth White had gotten herself into. At the most, the tunnels of the "D" train were pregnant with death and who knew what else.

"Listen, Digger, if it's the morphine she really went down there for . . . if Beth is really selling morphine . . . or giving it away . . . we can find it."

"How?"

"Bernstein."

"You mean your dog?"

84

"Right. Remember how Bernstein used to make his living—with his nose."

"But that was sniffing out undercover cops with wires. This is dope."

"He can learn quick. I can teach him quick."

"You're an actress, not a dog trainer."

"Six of one, half dozen of another."

"You mean that we all go down into the tunnel—you, me, and the dog?"

"Right."

"I'm a thief," he noted.

"And only one of the thieves were saved," I reminded him.

13

I used to have an acting teacher—his name was Bobby Segal—and for a while I was desperately in love with him, although nothing came of it. I found out years later that he was gay.

Anyway, he used to talk a lot about that indescribable quality called stage presence . . . or the power to transform others, fellow actors and audience alike . . . the power to elicit.

"Stage presence," he would say, "is like the Holy Ghost in Gerard Manley Hopkins' poem, 'God's Grandeur.'"

And then he would recite it, emphasizing the lines, "Because the Holy Ghost over the bent / World broods with warm breast and with ah! bright wings . . ."

He would say: "You have to feel that sense of covering the entire stage, the entire audience, the entire city. You have to feel that sense that every word and gesture . . . every flap of your bright wings will cause immense ripples."

Well, that was the way I felt after Patrice and I made love that night.

But it wasn't from the sex. It was from the warm, quiet feeling that I was hovering over Hell's Kitchen . . . that both what I knew and what I was about to know was so important that I held the fate of the neighborhood and perhaps the city in my hands.

His face was on my stomach. I played with his gray-black hair.

"What are you doing, Sally?"

"What am I doing? I'm running my fingers through your grizzled hair. Isn't that what lovers are supposed to do?"

"You know what I mean."

"No, I don't."

"I mean, what are you up to? You aren't around anymore. It's almost impossible to get you on the phone. You're up to something."

For a moment, for a very brief moment, I had the delicious feeling that I wanted to tell him . . . that I wanted him to know what I had found . . . that I wanted him to be dazzled, to be overwhelmed by the facts and by my efforts. But I held off.

"I'm trying to get back into some kind of pattern—you know, classes, auditions, contacts," I said, lying with equanimity.

"Something else is going on."

"What? Another man? Are you jealous, Patrice?"

"I don't know."

I laughed and pulled his ears.

"Sometimes," he said, "you treat me like one of your dogs. You ought to remember I'm much older than them. And I'm not a stray."

"And sometimes," I replied, "you treat me like an urban renewal project—like you're going to gentrify me."

"I guess," he mused, "it's better you treat me like one of your dogs than as one of your homeless friends."

"What do you mean by that?"

"Nothing, really. I was just thinking of that guy you told me about—who was murdered."

"Charlie Seven."

"Well, how did you treat him?"

"We weren't lovers, Patrice. We were friends. I realize that the concept of friendship is probably foreign to you. After all, when they take away all your club memberships, you're just a landlord."

He laughed and moved his head away from my hands, turning so he could look at me full face.

"No, it wasn't just friendship, Sally."

"How the hell would you know?" His arrogance infuriated me.

"One of my intuitions."

"You mean like your intuition that Hell's Kitchen would be a paradise on earth once the bodegas started selling sushi?"

The scream of a fire engine interrupted our increasingly hostile dialogue. The dogs ran to the windows, their tails high and waving (except for Heineken, who only had a stub of a tail left). Then they began to howl—like beserk bells, one after another. We both started to laugh. Then we howled along with them to the best of our ability. And then we made love again.

When we finished, and lay exhausted in each other's arms, I stared past his shoulder at the dogs. They were sitting on their haunches around us, in a semicircle, not sexually excited as they usually were in the face of human sexuality, but almost pensive. Molson, particularly, focused his immense bleary eyes on me.

"What the hell are they looking at?" Patrice asked.

Their gaze disturbed me. They were looking at me as if I had somehow betrayed them. It was not jealousy; it was hurt.

Patrice's body was totally relaxed. He put his face in my hair.

"I want you to move in with me," he whispered, "and you can bring all the dogs. I want to be with you all the time."

"I can't," I said, "I have things to do."

He wrapped his arms around me and pressed hard. I found myself unable to breathe and struggled free.

"In the spring, maybe in the spring," I said. He moved quickly off the mattress and began to dress.

When Digger came over, about noon, he was surly, and he wanted the rest of his money.

"Have you gone through all that money already?" I asked, astonished.

"No, I'm investing it."

"In hookers, no doubt," I parried.

"Look, I found Mrs. Toast for you," he said.

"Right. But you still have to find Arthur and Sleepy to get that last payment."

He shook his head sadly, as if it were impossible to deal with me. Then he asked: "What the hell am I doing here, anyway?"

"You're supposed to take four of my dogs for a walk so I can train Bernstein to sniff morphine."

"You really going through with it?"

"Yes. You, me, and Bernstein are going down into that subway tunnel."

"Then I better take you to Nolan."

"Who's Nolan?"

"A guy I know . . . an old guy who used to work in the subway tunnels."

"Sure. Why not?"

Digger looked at me, still skeptical. He was, in spite of his trade, in spite of his malnutrition, in spite of all his lunatic street hangups—an impressive young man. "You know, Digger," I said, "you don't have to go to hookers."

"Stick with your own kind," he said, quickly and bitterly, and for a moment I thought he had misunderstood

89

me and thought I was offering him an alternative, rather than making a general statement that many women would find him attractive. But then I realized he was making a very subtle point—that hookers were thieves in a sense, just as he was.

Then he gathered the leashes and took four of the dogs out, leaving me alone with Bernstein.

Bernstein was very unhappy at being passed over for this walk, particularly because he was the only one left. But, being a gentleman, he didn't protest too much, whining only a few times. And Bernstein was surely a kindly beast—in fact, sometimes he was so gentle he acted like a bitch whose puppies consisted of all living things. For example, when my pack played in the loft—tearing around after each other and running over whoever was on the mattress—only Bernstein slowed up enough to make sure he didn't step on me. Nor would he step on any living thing if he had the option.

"Bernstein," I said, "you are going to have to help me out. You are going to have to learn how to sniff out morphine."

He cocked his head to one side, the way only German shepherds do, the ears twitching nervously, the eyes moving across my face like radar antennae. God, he was handsome and full-boned. His head looked like it should be on a box of cereal.

I had the training material all ready, having constructed the simplest plan I could. Of course I hadn't the slightest idea how real dog trainers operate—but I wasn't too impressed with them. If I could housebreak five strays, I could do anything.

Actually, my training material consisted of 1) the used morphine syrettes, which I had broken open, and 2) a few cans of sardines in olive oil.

As for the sardines—well, there's a story behind them. Some months before I had been visited by an old friend, Bo Seixas. I was then still living in my old apartment. Bo lived in the Village but was uptown for an audition. She brought some sandwiches and soft drinks with her, but we became so engrossed in seeing each other, in trading gossip about who's doing what, that we forgot completely about the food.

Finally, when we got around to eating, we discovered that the sandwich bag had been raided. Someone or something had opened the bag, removed the wax paper and attacked only one sandwich—the sardine and raw onion on whole wheat. The culprit had carefully removed only the sardines and left the rest alone.

Light-pawed Bernstein—he was the culprit. And that was the way I discovered that what Bernstein loved most in life were sardines in olive oil—not necessarily skinless and boneless.

So, the pedagogical scheme was set out. The sardines were in my pocket, in an open can, but tightly wrapped with aluminum foil to diminish the odor.

The syrettes had been broken open and scattered throughout the apartment.

One was placed in full view of my storeroom/closet, sitting on a suitcase.

The second was in the bathroom, stuffed under a sink.

The third was in the kitchen sink, wrapped in a paper napkin.

I began the training program, tentatively named "The Sally Tepper Sardines and Narcotics Training Program for Low-Intelligence German Shepherds."

First, I led Bernstein into the storeroom/closet and showed him the syrette lying on the suitcase.

"*Morphine*," I said to him, repeating it three times and making sure he had a good sniff. I repeated the word "morphine" again and again while petting him profusely and telling him what a wonderful, beautiful, brave doggie he was.

I could tell he was beginning to get a whiff of the hidden sardines.

Then I walked out of the storeroom and waited ten minutes.

"Morphine," I called to Bernstein, who was then stretched out. He stood up, shook himself, and followed me into the storeroom. I called out "Morphine," showed him the syrette, and praised and scratched him effusively.

I did that three more times.

On the fourth try I just called out: "Bernstein, find the *morphine*, find the *morphine*."

Bernstein trotted into the storeroom and stood over the broken syrette. I walked in and gave him two large, luscious, oily sardines. He wolfed them down, licked his chops for every bit of the salty oil on his whiskers, and then just purred.

That was it for a while. When Digger came back with the other dogs, he asked: "Start the training?"

"Finished it."

He looked at me like I was crazy.

"Watch, Digger, watch."

I walked over to the closet and closed the door. Then I walked into the center of the room.

"Bernstein, come here," I said. The dog came. "Find the *morphine*, Bernstein, find the *morphine*."

He positively grinned as shepherds do, with the whole face, obviously thinking of more sardines. He trotted to the closet only to find to his utter dismay that the door was closed.

He pawed at the door. It wouldn't open.

"Bernstein, find the *morphine*. Find the *morphine*."

It dawned on him that the sardine bait was elsewhere. He began to sniff along the walls, and then went into the bathroom. Once he stepped on the tile floor, his whole body quivered for an instant and then he exploded toward the sink, desperately scratching at something with his paws, growling, biting at the plumbing.

"Help him out, Digger, help him out."

Digger walked into the bathroom and knelt beside the

dog. He laughed like a kid when he pulled out the broken syrette that had been stuffed under the sink.

I gave Bernstein three greasy sardines.

"That's unbelievable," Digger admired.

"Bernstein's a genius, Digger, didn't you know that?"

Bernstein found the paper-wrapped syrette in the kitchen sink almost as fast.

"I thought," Digger said, "it takes months to train drug-sniffing dogs."

"But, Digger, this is Hell's Kitchen."

Digger took me to see the man called Nolan at about four. We walked into a coffee shop on 49th Street and Tenth Avenue. We sat at the counter and had coffee.

"Where is he?" I asked, looking around.

"He ain't here," Digger said, blowing into his cup, "he's in a bar around the corner. I just wanted to warn you that he's a bit weird before you met him."

"What do you mean, weird?"

"Well, his head's not screwed on tight," Digger explained, "like a lot of those old Hell's Kitchen guys who used to work for the Transit Authority. In the old days, I heard, there were only two kinds of jobs in the neighborhood—on the docks or in the subways. A lot of the Irish guys went down in the subway. The Transit Workers Union was always an Irish union. I heard Nolan would drill and bolt and weld the third rail when the power was on. Maybe he stayed down too long—I'm just warning you. I mean, we ought to talk to him. He knows the tunnels, but he is weird."

"OK, Digger, let's get it over with. It's your idea."

We left the coffee shop and walked west until we reached a bar with no name. It just said BAR in broken neon over the large wooden door. Digger walked in and I followed him.

The place was filled with filtered blue light and good-looking black women dressed to kill.

We walked through the main area into a small alcove with chairs and tables, filled by old white men.

"There's Nolan," Digger whispered.

"What's going on in front? A convention?" I asked.

"Transvestites," Digger said, laughing nervously.

I turned and stared. I knew there were several transvestite bars in the neighborhood, but I had never been in one and I didn't know they were segregated by race. The transvestites were scarcely talking, lined up along the bar, one more baroque than another, smoking long brown cigarettes and drinking from tall glasses. They wore a profusion of hats.

We slid into chairs. Nolan was a small man with few teeth left, an incredibly lined face, and two enormous tufts of sandy hair that jutted out from each side of his otherwise bald head. He was wearing a filthy white shirt and a dark blue tie. His fingers were stumpy and stained yellow from nicotine.

"So, you're the writer, huh?" Nolan said, sloshing the whiskey in his tall glass.

"Writer?" I looked at Digger. He winked. I understood. Digger had told Nolan I was a writer; I was writing some kind of article for some kind of magazine on the subways.

"Well, there's nothing to worry about, honey. It's just a goddamn tunnel. Hell, they last forever. They were built eighty years ago. You wanna walk down there? Go ahead. You just walk. You want to climb out? Hell, there's all kinds of escape hatches and vents. You can climb right up to the street."

He finished his whiskey with a gulp and pointed the glass at Digger, who took it, left, and returned with it full . . . also bringing a glass of club soda and two steins of beer.

Nolan grabbed the fresh glass with both hands and sipped the whiskey. He bent over close to me, so close I could see the tiny specks of red in his blue eyes.

"You think the subway tunnels are the only ones down

94

there? Hell, there are a million tunnels under there—subway tunnels, phone cables, sewers—it's like a goddamn swiss cheese down there."

Two transvestites walked past us to the bathrooms in the rear. One of them waved at Nolan, who spat on the floor. The other blew him a sardonic kiss.

"I should still be down there," he said.

Digger smiled and sipped his beer. I left my beer alone. The juke box went on: Betty Carter, the jazz singer, singing a song I had never heard before.

"But I lost my goddamn nerve," Nolan continued, "I wasn't too old, I just lost my nerve. You know what I mean, honey?"

"Digger told me what you used to do," I replied. "It sounds like it was a very dangerous job."

"No! It wasn't the job. Hell, the job was a piece of cake if you knew what you were doing. It was the cats!"

"The cats?"

He bent over the table, talking lower, in a conspiratorial tone.

"The tunnel cats. They're big and savage and they have scabs all over their body and rabies. They've been down there for generations."

"I thought those stories were all fake," I said, looking around nervously for Digger's support.

"Fake? Real, honey, real as you. They're all blind, but they don't need eyes down there. They feed on rats and garbage and each other. But they love human meat best. They love to take a chunk out of you. And they carry disease in their filthy claws."

I sat back in my chair.

His words froze me with fear. I could see the cords of his neck knot.

"I could show you my chest," he whispered, "but I'm ashamed. I could show you where they clawed me . . . how they almost killed me."

I could feel one of my legs trembling.

Nolan grabbed my wrist and pulled me close to him, whispering in my ear: "They clawed my eyes out. These are not my eyes. The cats got them in the tunnel."

I pushed him away. I suddenly realized that Nolan was mad as a hatter. I looked at Digger. His face was averted.

It dawned on me that Digger had set me up with this lunatic to frighten me out of going down into the tunnel. I kicked him hard under the table and half his beer sloshed over the side.

"Good try, Digger," I said.

Nolan started to unbutton his shirt.

"Why don't *you* check his chest out, Digger? I'll meet you outside."

I walked past the transvestites and out on the street. It was beginning to sleet.

14

You think Bernstein would like some Remy?"

"If you put sardines in it."

We were perched on window ledges in my loft—Digger on one, me on an adjoining one.

It was thirty minutes to midnight.

We were drinking Remy in paper cups. I figured that since we were about to undertake a great adventure, we ought to toast our daring and, as they used to say in King Solomon's Mines, our "resolve."

The dogs were scattered throughout the loft. Bernstein was fast asleep on his side, his paws quivering in a dream . . . maybe about sardines and morphine.

"You know, Sally, it's not too late."

"For what?"

"To not go."

"Look, Digger, you don't want to go, I'll go alone."

"No! Just tell me the real goddamn reason we're going down there. It sure can't be just to find some morphine syrettes being retailed by a crazy, fat ex-nun."

I sipped the brandy. It was delicious. I stared down at the street, covered with a very thin blanket of ice.

There was no doubt that I owed Digger a good explanation. But there was nothing I could really articulate.

I knew I wasn't going down there to find morphine. I was going down to find Beth White's madness. For something had surely happened to her so profound, so ugly, that she was willing to debase the very people she had lived for.

And I wasn't going down there to find more homeless corpses. I was going down to put myself in danger, to somehow participate in all those deaths . . . to somehow share Charlie Seven's crucifixion.

I was going down there because I had uncovered a secret and I didn't know what the hell to do with it . . . *but I had to do something*.

I was like an archeologist who had discovered a lost language and was now searching for the society that had used it.

Digger poured more brandy into my cup. He was getting agitated. He was getting that street look on his face, as if he were looking for a fight.

I suddenly felt very sad that Digger really didn't want to go down there. Digger above all should have known that it was all about Hell's Kitchen. We had found out something that explains Hell's Kitchen. We had uncovered something horrible that was radiating out through the city, like the "D" train—something that went to the heart of the matter. We had our ears right at the heartbeat, as no one else ever had.

I looked at the clock. It was ten minutes past midnight.

"Time?" Digger asked.

"It's late enough," I replied.

We leashed Bernstein, threw the other dogs some tid-bits, and left the loft.

Digger and I were dressed as if we were going on an Alpine expedition, but the closer I came to that subway tunnel, the more I felt it was some kind of pilgrimage to a wise man, a guru, who lived in the tunnel . . . and he and only he could bring us the final enlightenment. He would make the waters clear . . . he would clarify . . . he would bring together the disparate elements and make sense out of them. And all we needed were subway tokens.

When we got to the platform we waited for a train to pull in and then pull out. Then we waited for another one . . . and another one . . . the time between each arrival lengthening as we entered the early morning hours.

We simply were afraid to go down into the tunnel.

"Either we go down or we go up," Digger finally said. His logic was impeccable.

I walked to the end of the platform and peered out into the tunnel. It was too dark to see clearly.

I grasped Bernstein by the collar and walked down the steps, onto the tracks. Digger followed us.

I moved only a foot or two, then stopped.

"We have to wait until our eyes get accustomed to the dark," I said to Digger.

We waited. It was cold. Gradually I could see that I was not standing on the track bed but on a raised cement walkway that bordered the tracks. It was narrow.

I started to walk. I could hear my heart beating in my chest. It sounded like a clock. In the distance, signals flashed. There was a strange, damp smell in the air.

Bernstein heeled without being asked; he didn't seem to be enjoying himself.

A train came through, going the other way on the far tracks. There was no danger, but the sudden explosion of light and screeching noise frightened us so much we pressed ourselves against the damp cold walls.

Then we walked on. The tunnel widened and we entered a gravel path along the rails. Above us were signal casings and transformer boxes.

Cold. Dark. Wet. Slivers of light bouncing around. Strange sounds. Rails humming and groaning. A sense of constriction and expansion, as if the tunnel were narrowing and widening in response to our breathing.

"Sally, look!" Digger's strained voice came from behind my shoulder.

"Where?"

"Right above your goddamn head."

I stared up.

The top of the tunnel was crisscrossed by steel grates. Through the grates I could make out massive cables. And above them, I could make out another grating and the street.

My shoulder hit something along the wall. It was a retractable ladder. I realized that one could climb from the tunnel to the street. Was that what Beth White had done?

It was time to go to work. I knelt beside Bernstein and pulled one of his ears.

"*Morphine*," I said.

He licked my nose.

"Morphine, Bernstein," I whispered into his ear hoarsely, "find the morphine and I'll give you two dozen sardines."

I accentuated "morphine" and "sardines." I unhooked the leash from the collar.

He bolted across the tracks toward the third rail.

"BERNSTEIN!" I yelled.

He stopped, wheeled, and stared. He was playing. He bounded back to me. He was ready to work.

Bernstein started moving along the wall. We followed. My hands and feet were becoming numb. The small flashlight I had brought along was not strong enough to totally illuminate Bernstein. I was frightened and miserable. I wished at that moment, very much, that Patrice were with me. I chastised him silently for not knowing and not caring . . . for not being with me . . . for not being trust-worthy enough to confide in . . . for not being what I wanted.

"Do you think he got it?" Digger whispered.

Digger meant the scent of morphine. I didn't know, but Bernstein was moving strongly, his tail high. He seemed to know where he was going and what he was doing.

Then he vanished from sight. I stopped and waited. He didn't show. I couldn't hear him.

"Did he go on the tracks?" Digger asked.

"No, just deeper into the tunnel, along the wall."

I kept calling him in a low, desperate voice.

He reappeared suddenly, panting. The lower part of his body was coated with water, mud, and slime.

"Hold his collar," Digger called.

I grasped the collar and Bernstein moved forward again. The wall we were walking along suddenly vanished to reveal another set of tracks.

"It's where they hold trains or lay them up," Digger speculated.

We moved across this new set of tracks. Water was everywhere, dripping from overhead pipes.

Bernstein suddenly broke loose from my grip. He darted forward with a little bark.

"He's got it, Sally, he's got it," Digger yelled excitedly into my ear.

When we caught up with Bernstein, he was standing in front of a large white steel door built into the wall of the tunnel—on which was stenciled: DANGER. HIGH VOLT-AGE.

Digger cursed and stamped his feet.

He said: "Your stupid dog is supposed to sniff out morphine, not electrical substations. Maybe he's an elec-tricity freak. Maybe he gets off on high voltage."

I grabbed his collar and bent down beside him. "Bernstein, is it *morphine—morphine.*"

He whined and strained at the collar.

"This place is strange, Digger."

"What's strange? It's a goddamn electrical substation. Switches, generators . . . they're all over the subways."

"I mean these tracks."

Digger stared around.

"They haven't been used for a long time," I noted.

"So what?"

"And look at those water pipes overhead, dripping all over the tracks."

"I repeat. So what?"

"Why would they keep an electrical substation on a stretch of waterlogged abandoned tracks?"

"I think where they place them has to do with distance . . . or something else. It doesn't matter where they're placed."

"Get me a piece of wood, Digger."

"What for?"

"To open it."

"You don't want to do a stupid thing like that, Sally."

"I don't *want* to do it, Digger, but I'm going to do it."

"Where do I get wood?"

"Along the tracks."

He cursed and sloshed off. I kept ahold of Bernstein, calming him down. Digger came back with two slats of wood.

I chose the shorter, stronger piece, inserted it between the steel door and the wall, jerked hard and jumped back.

The door opened.

We stared in astonishment. There were no switches! There were no transformers!

It was a dummy!

The only thing we saw was a spiral staircase, made of a kind of steel webbing.

I poked my head inside and stared upward. The staircase, I realized, had to go to the street, but only two or three landings were visible.

Bernstein was beginning to pull and whine and prance.

"He's onto it," Digger said, "but how do we get him up the steps?"

They were narrow and wet and treacherous looking.

"Let's just make it to the first landing," I said. "You push from behind and I'll pull from the front."

Up we went, slowly, holding on to each other and the stair railing tightly.

We rested, huddled close together on the landing. I threw the beam around the four walls.

The light fell on a strange, half-obscured symbol, high up on the wall.

I looked at it and then laughed out loud.

"What's so funny?" Digger asked.

"I think we're in an old bomb shelter," I whispered.

The symbol on the wall was a black triangle in a yellow circle.

It was the old Civil Defense symbol that used to mark school bomb shelters during the heyday of the Cold War and the nuclear scares. I hadn't seen one since I was a very little girl, in kindergarten.

Bernstein was almost uncontrollable now, pulling against his collar and making all kinds of groaning noises, as if I were preventing him from getting water on a hot day.

I inched over to the wall. My hands slid along it. My fingers caught a niche . . . a recess.

They weren't solid walls, I realized. They were closets.

I pulled at the panel. It opened very slowly, ever so slowly, as if the rollers had never been caked with a lubricant.

"Digger! Look!"

The closet was packed with plain wooden boxes . . . each one the size of a small footlocker.

Bernstein stuck his nose inside—growling.

There were two rows of boxes.

One contained morphine syrettes. The other contained packaged dressings.

"It's a pusher's paradise," Digger said.

Half the morphine boxes in the first row were empty. The boxes with the medical dressings had not been touched.

Bernstein started to paw me. He had done his job. He wanted his sardines. But I had forgotten to bring them.

"Where's this stuff from? Who put it here?" Digger asked.

I shined the light far back into the closet. What I thought was a shallow closet was really a deep vault. There were hundreds of boxes, probably containing hundreds of thousands of morphine syrettes and an equal number of dressings.

I moved to the next wall. It was a vault, also. The boxes in it were untouched.

I opened one. Inside were hundreds of packets of dried milk powder.

The other boxes contained all manner of dried foods—beans, eggs, rice, cocoa.

Untouched, piled high, piled deep, were enough basic nutrients to feed a small city.

I moved to the next wall. It, too, opened like a closet.

Again the boxes. I opened one. Inside were pamphlets with plain gray covers. I shined the light on one.

The title was: EMERGENCY SANITARY PROCEDURES IN ZONE OF ATOMIC IMPACT. It was odd to see the old word "atomic," which has since given way to the term "nuclear."

I opened another box. It, too, had pamphlets—but different ones. The title was: EMERGENCY MEDICAL TREATMENT OF RADIATION BURNS.

All the pamphlets had the imprint of the Surgeon General's Office of the U.S. and the Department of Defense. All were printed by the Government Printing Office in Washington, D.C., between 1954 and 1957.

The final closet contained equipment and pills for purifying water.

I moved away from the closets and squatted, holding Bernstein tightly. I was suddenly exhausted.

"This is incredible, Digger," I said.

"Yeah, but what is all this?"

"It must have been stored here in the 1950s . . . in case of a nuclear attack."

"By who?"

"The Government, I guess. And the City. I don't know who did it. But the purpose is obvious—food, medicine, instructions for survivors."

"Hell, it makes sense," Digger said. "I mean, if you're going to hide this stuff—you might as well hide it in the subway. I mean, if they ever drop one of those bombs on New York, the only thing left will probably be the subway . . . at least the tunnels."

Bernstein moaned. Poor dog. He had earned his sardines. And I couldn't give him any.

We huddled in silence on the landing for a long time, gathering our strength. We were all breathing heavily.

Digger tried to light a cigarette, but his matches were too wet. He let out a string of low ugly curses.

"Now we know about the 'D' train, don't we, Digger?"

"Know what?"

"If they stored that stuff down here, they must have many other storage points in the subway."

"And the 'D' train runs as the crow flies . . . underground," Digger said, excited.

"Right. From the tip of the Bronx to the tip of Brooklyn. It's a perfect distribution network. The backbone of the city, and at each vertebra, a storage dump."

"But why not the other subway lines?"

"Probably them, too," I said, "but the 'D' train is the only one we have proof for."

"What proof? We have only one, and one storage dump don't mean a thing."

"Remember all those murders, Digger. All along the 'D' line. I think that where there were corpses, there was morphine."

"I think we ought to get the hell out of here and pay a visit to that fat nun," Digger said.

"*Ex*-nun, Digger, she's an ex-nun," I corrected.

15

When we got back to the loft the first thing I did was take a hot shower. Then I gave Bernstein more sardines than he had ever seen, much less consumed, in his life.

Digger went to sleep on the long, beat-up secondhand sofa, which had become one of my proudest new acquisitions.

Bernstein, after the sardines, collapsed.

The other dogs just stared, bleary-eyed, at all the commotion.

I got dressed in dry clothes and made coffee—waking Digger when I had poured his cup. The clock read 2:15 AM. It was amazing. We had only been in the subway tunnel for about an hour. It felt like we had been down there the entire night.

I gave Digger a whole bunch of dry shirts—half mine, half Patrice's—to try on. He stripped to the waist and tried on one after another. It was astonishing how skinny Digger was without his shirt on. His ribs stuck through his chest like acorns.

Finally, one flannel shirt vaguely fit, and he buttoned it up.

Digger started to doze over his coffee.

"Look, Digger, why don't you stay here if you're tired."

He snarled at me. I changed the subject. I wasn't tired at all. In fact I felt light and strong and smart. It was like being given a script to read and knowing, even before the script was opened, the role to be played.

"Where's the brandy?" Digger asked.

"In the kitchen."

He brought back the bottle of Remy and a bottle of ale from the kitchen. He took a swallow from the brandy and then from the ale. He repeated the drink once more, then lit a cigarette.

"I'm ready," he said.

"In a minute," I replied, and took a comb to my hair to get the tunnel knots out.

"My brother used to hate red-haired women," Digger noted.

"Is that so?"

"Yeah. He said they were all frigid."

"What does your brother know?"

Digger laughed. "Maybe not much."

He took another swallow of the brandy and the ale.

I wondered what would happen to Digger. What eventually happened to low-level thieves? Jail? Alcoholism? Suicide? Insanity? Sometimes, when I looked at him, I could see him emerging as Charlie Seven. It was odd how all the men I knew were now somehow tied into a fantasy world that included that poor sad man.

"What are you staring at?" he asked aggressively.

"You."

"Lose something here?"

"Not really. I was just thinking about your future."

This struck Digger as enormously funny. He laughed so loud that Budweiser woke up and ambled over to see if he was OK. He offered her the bottle of brandy. She sniffed and walked away.

"You know, I shoulda took a few hundred of those syrettes. Hell, I earned them."

"But, Digger, you're a good guy now."

"There are no good guys. No bad guys. Just thieves and fences. Fences and thieves."

"Beth White is a bad guy, Digger. Anyone who gives desperate people morphine is bad."

"You mean Mrs. Toast."

"And God knows who else she gave them to."

"Or sold them."

"Right. Or sold them."

"What did the old lady pay with? Two pieces of rye toast?"

"That's what we're going to find out at the League offices."

"Why don't we wait till the morning? How do we know they're there?"

I could not restrain my cynicism. "Always there, Digger. Always open. That's what the League for the Homeless is all about—*sanctuary*."

We left the loft and walked to the League storefront. As usual, it was brightly lit.

"I don't see anyone inside," Digger said.

"Beth sleeps there, Digger, and so do a lot of other people."

We crossed the street, opened the door, and walked in. Everything was as usual—desks, phones, chairs, cartons, leaflets.

We heard sounds, voices, coming from the adjoining room, where the cots were usually set up, and through which one had to walk to reach the bathroom and the kitchen.

I heard Beth's voice distinctly, from behind the door. It was unmistakable.

"What do we do now?" Digger whispered.

I signaled with my arm that he should keep quiet.

Beth's voice was clearer. She wasn't speaking; she was reciting.

I listened.

"God chose the foolish things of the world to shame the wise men . . . And God chose the feeble things of the world to shame the mighty . . .

"And God chose the insignificant things of the world and the despised—the 'nothings'—in order that he might nullify the existing things . . . So that no human may glory before God."

I held on to Digger, pressing my fingers into his arm. Her hypocrisy overwhelmed me. She was spouting St. Paul's First Corinthians and stuffing morphine into old ladies. I hated her at that moment with such an intensity that I could scarcely stand.

"What do you want to do?" Digger whispered.

Someone else now was speaking from the other room. It sounded like Allissandro, but I couldn't be sure—the words were blurred.

"Man, we can't stay here," Digger pleaded, "let's get in or get out."

I opened the door and walked through—Digger following.

I saw Beth and Allissandro first. They didn't greet us. They were standing beside a folding table; on it were small packets.

I picked one up and turned it over in my hand. It was a sewing kit. I dropped it quickly when I realized it was the exact same kind of packet Charlie Seven had given me as a belated Christmas present.

The room was strangely quiet. But the chairs and the cots were filled with homeless people.

Mrs. Toast was there. She regarded me calmly. I

searched quickly for other familiar faces—thinking for a moment that the missing members of Charlie Seven's family, Sleepy and Arthur, would be there with Mrs. Toast. They were not.

Something was very disturbing about the atmosphere. Something was just too odd. I felt like a disruptive intruder—like a thief. Digger brought me back to reality.

"It's a goddamn sewing circle," he said.

And he was right. Each person in the room was calmly sewing a strange piece of white fabric. A shirt . . . those stupid white shirts with the buffalo design . . . the shirt that Charlie Seven supposedly had been wearing when he was murdered . . . shirts like we had found sticking out ludicrously under Mrs. Toast's sweaters.

I looked at Beth. She smiled grimly at me. Every feeling of affection I ever had for the woman dissolved in that instant.

"Saint Beth of Hell's Kitchen," I spat out, contemptuously, and swept the sewing packets off the table with my open palm.

My whole body was suddenly trembling with rage. I fought to control myself.

"We found your morphine, Beth," I said, "we followed you and we found it. But that's only a small part of it. Right? There are civil defense vaults from the 1950s up and down the subway system. Right? And you know them all, don't you, Beth? And you know about all those homeless murders up and down the 'D' train line. Don't you, Beth? And you know a lot more about Charlie Seven's murder, don't you, Beth?"

She backed away from me, her arms folded tightly as if she were in pain—her head shaking in violent denial.

"We saw you give Mrs. Toast the morphine, Beth. We saw you go into the tunnel."

"Sally, listen," she replied, staring at Allissandro and then at me, "I don't know anything about murder. About Charlie Seven's murder or anyone else's. And I don't know

about more vaults in the subway. There are no more—
except what you found. That's the only place I ever took
those syrettes from."

"You're lying, Beth. Your whole life's a lie, a fake, a
con. You're the Angel of Death."

Then she screamed at me: "Why would I kill Charlie?
Why would any of us here kill Charlie Seven? He was part
of our church."

I stepped back—startled. Church? What was she talking about?

I looked at Mrs. Toast. She still sat calmly.

"Charlie Seven belonged to no church."

"He belonged to my church," Allissandro affirmed.

"Your church?"

"If you compose yourself, Sally. If you stop making
those crazy accusations against Beth—I can explain."

"By all means explain," I said.

Allissandro walked into the front office. Beth followed, then Digger, then myself. The door between the
two rooms was left open. From where I seated myself I
could see the homeless people, still seated, still sewing their
absurd shirts.

Digger lit a cigarette. He kept looking at me with dis-
gust, as if I had embroiled him in something he could not
tolerate.

"Do you know how long Beth and I have worked
here?" Allissandro asked.

"I don't know. And I don't really care."

"Twenty years," he said, answering his own question,
"and for those twenty years we did our best. What was our
best? Feed some people. Bury some people. Clothe some
people. Help the homeless and the derelicts get from day
to day . . . season to season. Nothing ever changed."

"Except death," Beth interjected. "There is more of
it. Everything is uglier and harsher."

"You don't understand, Sally," Allissandro continued,

"you have other interests. But Beth and I confronted it twenty-four hours a day for twenty years."

"Get to the point," I said, nastily, not wanting him to dilute my focus.

"About a year ago, things became very bad. Very bad. We could not raise enough money. We could not provide enough services. We could not—"

Allissandro stopped in the middle of his narrative. He walked over to Beth and grasped her hand. Then he stared at me intently and said: "It was then that I had the vision."

"The vision?"

I was becoming uneasy, very uneasy. Something was surfacing for which I was in no way prepared.

"Yes, a vision. Perhaps not the kind of vision that was received at Lourdes or Fatima. No, it wasn't a sudden blinding visitation by the Son of God or the Mother of God. No . . . it wasn't that."

Allissandro released Beth's hand. She seemed to hover over him, to envelop him. He stepped away, looked past me, into the other room, at the sewing circle.

"Tell her," Beth said.

He smiled at the ex-nun. He spoke quietly but with great passion.

"I realized that the homeless state is the one most beloved by God.

"I understood that the men, women, and children who lived and died on our streets were put there by God to illuminate the ugliness and evil of our society. It was made clear to me that this society, as we know it, will be utterly destroyed.

"I realized that the homeless must seek no shelter . . . must seek no help. They must accept their state as beloved of God because when the city is destroyed for its indifference and its wealth and its arrogance—only they in their innocence would survive."

His voice had become so impassioned I could no

longer look at him. I looked at Digger who seemed to be in a state of discomfort bordering on shock.

Allissandro touched me on the face as if I were a communicant. I hit his hand away and then recoiled from my violence—as if I had struck a holy man.

He continued: "They must wait and suffer in silence and love. That is why they were given the morphine . . . to ease their pain while they waited. It was God's providence . . . His will . . . which revealed that store of morphine for us. In all the vast tunnels of the subway system, a single source was revealed to us. Like manna in the wilderness.

"And they were given the task of sewing a special shirt, which will be a sign of their salvation when the apocalypse comes . . . death shall pass over them as it passed over the children of Israel in Egypt."

It became very quiet.

All I could hear was labored breathing and strange rustling sounds from the other room.

"Beth," I said, in an imploring voice, as if asking her for a recantation, as if asking her to assure me that all of this was some kind of joke, some kind of metaphor . . . a piece of street theater.

She looked at me defiantly. Allissandro looked at me with kindness, as if I were a poor dumb creature who would never be able to understand the vision. Digger looked at me as if he were surrounded by kooks. He lit a cigarette with a groan.

I sat down. His speech and Beth's affirmation had drained me. They had obviously crossed the line—the very thin and fragile line—between religious belief and sheer lunacy.

Oh, it was understandable. Of course it was understandable. Beth White and Robert Allissandro had been in the trenches for years. The city had finally deranged them. Their impotence, their failure to effect change had destroyed their reason. The pain they saw and felt and could not alleviate had finally broken their will.

If they could not transform the plight of the homeless and derelicts they would construct a rationale—that their plight was really no damn plight at all . . . *it was spiritual purity.*

I had heard it all before as a child: in Sunday school, in children's books, in the fantasies of cousins and friends, in the pot and mescaline culture of teenagers.

Allissandro's vision was a mishmash of themes. There was the biblical story of the Jews in Egypt . . . there was the prediction of Armageddon in the Book of Revelations.

And all of it was laid over, was pasted over, the last great apocalyptic religious revival of the American Indians in the West.

Incredulous at how the entire bizarre vision had become so clear to me, I stared at the two saviors of the homeless. It was, I realized, the American Indian connection that had been the lynchpin and that I had simply not understood or recognized before. But the connection had been there from the beginning right out in the open: the buffalo design and the strange shirt worn by both Charlie Seven and Mrs. Toast. How had I missed it? Was there ever a Hollywood Indian movie that had not featured it? Was there ever a book written about the American Indians that had not used it as a symbol? Was there ever a civil rights orator who had not paid tribute to the final pathetic struggle of the American Indians to survive as a people? As a people whose life was entwined with the life of the buffalo? My lack of perception and intuition appalled me.

Poor Beth and Allissandro—powered by Vatican II to preach and live the social gospel—had ended up embracing a bizarre struggle for national liberation from the nineteenth century, one that had been doomed before it started.

Didn't Allissandro understand where his "vision" had

come from? Didn't they all understand that this was New York City . . . *today*?

Didn't Allissandro and Beth and even the poor souls they had "converted" understand that the vision was a copy of the Ghost Dance religion among the "homeless" American Plains Indian tribes in the 1890s?

They, too, were hungry, restless, destroyed by alcohol and disease—their spirits broken, their culture forgotten. But then a prophet had risen among them preaching that all this misery would soon pass; that the apocalypse was coming and only they would survive and then the buffalo would reappear on the great plains in their countless millions.

This prophet taught the Indians a dance and how to make a certain kind of shirt that would make them impervious to the bullets and diseases of the white man. The design on the shirt was some form of a buffalo skull.

Allissandro and Beth had appropriated that movement; only the dance was now morphine.

It was so sad. So stupid. I was so sick of it all. I hated such true believers.

I looked once again into the other room. God's morphine users seemed not to be aware of us; they continued their sewing, calm, quiet, waiting no doubt for the apocalypse that Allissandro had promised them . . . armed with the sure knowledge that God through Allissandro had decreed that only they would survive.

I cursed them under my breath. I cursed Allissandro and Beth. True believers all. While outside, without their calmness, the homeless littered the city—in hallways, in subways, under grates, in burned-out shells of buildings.

"What about the stray dogs?" I yelled my question angrily at Allissandro.

His face showed perplexity.

"The stray dogs. Aren't they beloved of God, also? Aren't you going to give them morphine also, to wait for the end? Won't they survive your apocalypse, too?"

Allissandro didn't answer.

"Aren't they beloved of God, also?" I repeated my question to Beth. She didn't answer.

I turned to Digger. "You see, Digger," I said, sarcastically, "the stray dogs don't fall under Allissandro's vision. We can't give them any morphine shots."

All Digger replied was: "Let's get out of here, Sally."

"I don't want to get out of here, Digger. I want to bask in his vision," I said. My anger was growing. The awesome stupidity of the whole mess was festering. Sure, the vision had come from Allissandro's heart. But it was corrosive. It was a vision for zombies.

I stared again at the sewers, sitting placidly, clumsily making their grotesque white shirts. Mrs. Toast had closed her eyes. She seemed to be sleeping.

"Tell me, Allissandro—when will this apocalypse arrive?" I asked.

"It was not given to me . . . the exact moment," he replied.

"Well—sooner or later?"

"I don't know."

"In a week? A year? Ten years?"

"I don't know."

"What kind of apocalypse will it be?"

"I don't know."

"A nuclear attack? An earthquake? A flood? A plague? What?"

I wanted to interrogate him out of his vision. I wanted to shake his confidence. I wanted to humiliate him, to browbeat him, to loosen the foundation of his faith.

But it was futile. He stared at me tenderly as if I were the poor fool. Even Beth began to give me the cow eyes of the true believer—"Soon you, too, will believe, and we are here to help you," her eyes said.

"Beth," I said, "look! Look into that room. It isn't a church, Beth, it's a morphine ward."

Beth shook her head sadly at my persistent ignorance and my inability to understand.

Something in me snapped then. It all seemed to come together in one gush of rage.

I walked into the other room and stared at the homeless people. They stared back at me—friendly, waiting.

I knelt beside Mrs. Toast. The old woman inclined her head toward me as if I were about to say something private . . . as if she wanted me to say something.

"Come home with me, Mrs. Toast."

"I can't, Dearie," she whispered.

"Charlie wouldn't have wanted you here," I said.

"Charlie *is* here," she replied, "and he is such a nice man, such a very nice man."

I stood up. They kept on sewing . . . all of them.

I walked up to a young man with a purple gash across his face and ripped the shirt out of his hand. He looked at me and smiled.

From one to the other I went—ripping those stupid shirts out of their grasps.

Faster and faster. I began to race around the room, gathering them up, piling them in my arms. I began to hear screams and shouts.

There was a pressure on my arm—tighter and tighter. I found it harder to move. My chest was heaving. It was hard to breathe.

Suddenly I was staring at Digger. His fingers were digging into my arm.

"Easy, easy, be cool, Sally," he pleaded.

I tried to break free. The shirts were now heavy in my arms. I was drenched with sweat.

"Get your hands off me," I said, and then repeated those words again and again until he reluctantly released his pressure on my arm.

I walked slowly back into the office and flung the shirts down in front of Allissandro and Beth.

"Burn them," I whispered. My voice was hoarse. I was trembling. They didn't respond.

"BURN THEM!" I screamed.

"We can't do that," Beth said.

My composure was coming back. Digger was now by my side. I held on to his arm.

"Then cut them in ribbons or stuff them down an incinerator or dye them blue and give them to the Salvation Army."

"They are visible signs of our church . . . of my vision," Allissandro said.

He had spoken very quietly, but I could hear the cracks in his voice; I could hear his dream crumbling. Had he really believed he was the Messiah of the Homeless? He looked around, as if hoping for an outside force to strike me down . . . to retrieve his vision. I hated him and pitied him. He closed his eyes. I could see the muscles of his jaw clenching.

I sat down. I realized that I had to be very precise. I had to spell it out. I closed my eyes and tried to relax, as if I were preparing to enter a role . . . as if I were preparing to slide into the heart and soul and language of another person.

When I was composed and strong, I spelled it out.

"Listen to me. Your church is now disbanded. You are never going to take another package out of that morphine cache. You are never going to distribute another sewing kit. You are never going to preach your apocalypse to the homeless again. Do you understand me?"

They looked at me blankly. It was hard to tell what they were thinking. I had to make it very simple . . . very very simple.

"If you don't do what I say, I'm going to walk into the station house on Fifty-fourth Street with some used syrettes and Mrs. Toast and they're going to arrest you and put you away for trafficking in morphine. Digger and I will swear you sold morphine to us. I will take them down into the subway tunnel to see the looted vault—and they'll get you also for breaking into government property and theft. The West Side League will be destroyed. Everything we have all worked for all these years will become ashes. The homeless will die in the streets without anyone giving a damn."

There was a strange sound from the other room. Someone was weeping or babbling. Beth's face looked ravaged, crumpled.

"I'm tired, Digger, take me home."

16

Two days? Three days? Five days? Who knows? The depression was disabling. I lay on the mattress in the loft and watched the dogs.

Depression hits everyone differently. With me it means I can only move with great difficulty. I get physically wiped out. I lie down and stay down. My arms weigh two hundred pounds each. Opening a can takes me all day— one turn of the opener every hour or so.

But something really strange happens to my head. Of course, I get a little suicidal and I cry a lot, but then there comes a kind of clarity; I can think in an abstract way; I sort of get out of myself . . . I lie there and can see myself.

Anyway, this depression, my post-"vision" depression, was like all the others—just a bit longer and a bit deeper.

I spent most of my time looking at the dogs. Each reacted to my depression in his or her own way.

Molson, of course, was predictable. He thought I was

doing just fine. Being so large, so confused, and so lazy, Molson thought all movement was stupid unless absolutely necessary. To get him to do anything was like pushing an elephant out of the traffic. So, when I more or less collapsed, Molson approved with constant groans.

Poor, frightened, catlike Stout was so confused by my depression that he interpreted it as mortal danger. He spent most of the day flying from one end of the loft to another at top speed, looking for a way out. Then he collapsed from exhaustion and slept, then started running again.

What a strange dog Stout is. I found him in Central Park, shivering under a broken stone wall along the 79th Street transverse. Every time I tried to approach him under that wall, he alternately cringed and bared his fangs. It took me hours to coax him out. Stout was the craziest, saddest dog I had ever found. He was so skinny he looked like a coat hanger. And he really never recovered from his stray life.

Budweiser was maternal, as usual, coming over from time to time to check out if I was still alive. Sometimes, as if I were an errant puppy, she would grasp my wrist gently in her mouth and pull at me.

Heineken used my depression to satisfy his insatiable curiosity, a curiosity I often had to curb by throwing something at him. For example, one couldn't shower without him trying to climb in; one couldn't cook without having him inspect all the ingredients; and one couldn't make love without having him decide that it should be a threesome instead of a twosome.

Well, this time he began to take advantage of my disability by a long, careful inspection of my slippers, my mattress, my closet, and every inch of the kitchen. God knows what he found out when he was out of my sight.

As for Bernstein, he just seemed to sit a lot, regally, as if he were posing for a dog magazine. Well, he was a

beautiful animal and he was a hero of the subway system—
the Master Morphine Sniffer.

Patrice was very understanding. He did put me
through a short telephone interrogation: Did I often suffer
from such bouts of depression? Was I going to a shrink?
Was I taking anything for it?

He wanted to help me. I told him just to let me be by
myself until it lifted. He didn't press any further. But he
did send me flowers every day. And he sent hot food from
various ethnic takeout places. He even paid for a dog-
walker, which was very uncomfortable to accept at first,
but which I did—and quickly grew out of my discomfort.

I missed Patrice, even when depressed. He had become a major part of my life. He had become more than
a lover—almost a safety net that I could always count on
to be there, to be supportive, to make all kinds of small
silly gestures that somehow made things better. But I didn't
want to see him during those days because he would want
to make love, and the first thing depression kills is Eros.

Then Digger paid me a visit. His first words when he
got into the loft were: "God, you look terrible."

I laughed. Here I was, at the end of a depression, just
coming out of it, and a malnourished thief is telling me
how bad I look.

"You sick?' he proceeded.

"A bit depressed," I said, "but getting better."

He had brought cheese for the dogs and I watched
him joyfully fling the slices up into the air and create absolute havoc among a pack of leaping, growling, whirling,
groaning, chomping beasts. Digger loved havoc.

When all the cheese was consumed he lit a cigarette,
sat down on the floor with his back against a wall, and said:
"I have decided not to take any more money from you.
Keep the last payment."

"That's very noble of you, Digger, but you haven't
earned your last payment."

123

"Well, what I mean is that I'll find Sleepy and Arthur for you free."

"It doesn't matter to me anymore."

"OK. I'll find them just for laughs."

"I'm tired of the whole mess, Digger."

"Yeah, it sure turned out strange."

"Not strange, Digger, wrong. I was wrong. Everything I figured out—from beginning to end—was wrong."

"You did pretty good," Digger said, in a pathetic attempt to make me feel intelligent.

"No, Digger, I was delusional."

"You were what?"

"My whole, carefully informed analysis was worthless. I discovered a pattern of murders—all connected—a grand conspiracy that no one could see but myself. There is none . . . there was none . . . except in my own head. We'll never know why those people were murdered . . . or why Charlie was murdered. There is no 'why.' It's just the city. Homeless die. Some freeze to death. Some are beaten to death. And a lot die along, under, and over the 'D' train . . . and the 'F' train and the 'E' train."

Digger made a motion with his hand, as if he wanted to slow down my self-criticism.

"And the morphine, Digger. Remember when we found the morphine? I put two and two together and knew that there was a series of vaults up and down the 'D' train . . . correlating to the murders. Another delusion. Beth said there was only one vault—and I believe her. It was probably just overlooked . . . left there by mistake when the rest of them were dismantled in the early 1960s. No murders, Digger. No correlations. No conspiracy. Just two crazy fools who had a crazy vision. Just another lunatic Hell's Kitchen hustle."

I was talking clearly, without passion, able to see in my weakness almost the entire range of my delusions. I felt nothing except a kind of weary clarity.

"Well, it all made sense to me," Digger said.

"At the time."

"Right, at the time. And backed up by all that bread . . . all that green," he added, his eyes twinkling.

"I'm glad I temporarily enlightened you, Digger. Now let's hope you didn't catch anything from all those hookers you frequented with my money."

Digger waved the concern aside. "What's going to happen to you now?" he asked.

"What do you mean?"

"I don't know. I'm starting to worry about you."

I looked at him in astonishment.

"*You* are worrying about *me*?"

"Right."

I must look really bad, I realized, for a crazy street hustler to be worrying about me.

"Well, why don't you marry the guy you're sleeping with?"

"I don't want to get married right now, Digger."

"Then act. You're an actress, right?"

"I'll think about it."

"You know, Sally, maybe you'll take me to acting classes. You think I could make it as an actor?"

"I don't know, Digger."

"Someone once told me I'd make a great actor."

"Who?"

"I think it was a cop." He laughed at his own joke. He loved his own jokes.

Digger may have made a good point. Thieves make good actors. They know how to usurp characters.

Then we sat in silence for a long time. He smoked and sang snatches of Jerry Lee Lewis songs and played with the dogs, who visited him frequently, hoping he still had some cheese left. He had none. Digger always burned his bridges behind him.

We heard the fire engines again—a now familiar wail—signifying another burning. Winter chimes in Hell's Kitchen.

"I think," I said, "that if one lives here long enough—in Hell's Kitchen—you tend to lose your ability to think. I mean, I think feverishly . . . I see things in bizarre colors. There is no calm. You know what I mean, Digger?"

Digger groaned and stood up. "Yeah, well . . . you're starting to talk that funny shit." He didn't like me to be philosophical. It bothered him.

"I'll be in touch," he added.

"You blow all the money?"

"Don't worry about a thing."

"Going back to being a thief?"

"Hell, a trade is a trade."

He walked toward me as if he were about to shake hands or kiss me. At the last moment he turned away, confused, unsure of himself, and just walked out of the loft.

I closed my eyes and thought of Beth White and Robert Allissandro. How does one dissolve a church? What could they do with the vision now? Was morphine addictive? What would happen to the poor, sad, homeless fools who had shot themselves full of happiness to wait for the apocalypse? Would Beth survive? Would the League survive? Would she go back to doing what she had always done? Bring hope to those on the bottom? Would I ever be able to have a stein of ale with her again in Amy's?

I napped and then woke, feeling much better, feeling the weight of the depression begin to lift from my limbs. The loft was taking shape. All I really needed to finish it up was to buy a bedstead on which to put the mattress.

Digger's visit had sort of warmed me. He was worried about me, obviously, and that was probably a new emotion for him. It was nice the way he had ordered me to get back into the theater, as if failure was my own choice. My career had been going downhill for years. I had taken one step up and then nine steps down.

The last good role I had, in fact, was three years ago in a workshop production of the Hudson Guild.

They were putting on three one-act plays by a new Puerto Rican playwright. The one I was in was called *Looking for Work*. It was about a young Hispanic man who goes for a job interview and is interviewed by a crazy Anglo lady—me.

I got the part probably because I was so far from being Hispanic—tall, statuesque (even buxom at that time), red-haired—that the director thought the juxtaposition would make the play more intense. He was right.

I closed my eyes and tried to remember the opening monologue of the one-act, my monologue. It was very funny and very sad at the same time. I was supposed to be one of those smart dumb blondes, like Judy Holliday or Marilyn Monroe . . . a character who speaks stupidly but utters all kinds of ludicrous insights.

When the curtain opened I was seated behind a desk doing my nails, wearing a very tight-fitting dress. In comes the Hispanic applicant. He is very nervous. I give him a long stare of almost contempt, then realize my professional responsibilities and say something like:

"I have absolutely nothing against you people, nothing at all. Why, I wouldn't serve a meal without at least one kind of Goya beans on the plate. And besides, I just love the way you talk . . . it sounds almost Italian."

The whole play was about thirty minutes long. It got wackier and wackier. And, at the end, my character is so distraught at not being able to place the young Hispanic in a job (he talks funny, dresses funny, eats funny food) that I begin to strip and end up on the desk, so that his trip to the office shouldn't be a total waste.

The three-play program was a hot ticket for about six weeks—and there was all kinds of talk around that it was going to open at a large Off-Broadway theater. But it was just talk. It soon faded from view and memory.

Thinking about that disappointment made me very sad. I got up very slowly and walked to the kitchen. There was still some brandy left. I drank it. The kitchen floor was filthy and there were all kinds of unwashed dishes in the sink. I made a mental note to do some cleaning when I was up to it.

As I walked out of the kitchen I saw the long cabinet door ajar. I peered in. What a bloody mess! Heineken must have gotten into the closet while I was disabled. He had removed all the plastic garbage bags from the carton; he had chewed the Brillo pads; he had created havoc.

"Bad dog, Heineken!" I shouted from the kitchen. All I heard in response from the back of the loft was the running feet of the criminal as he sought to hide from his crime and my wrath.

Then I just burst out laughing so hard I could hardly stand.

It had been a long time between laughs.

17

I think we're getting close to spring."

"I hate spring."

Patrice, who had been lying on his stomach, was so perplexed by my comment, he turned over.

"Sometimes, Sally, you're very perverse."

"Sexually?"

He laughed.

"No, not sexually." He put his thin, strong arm around me and pulled me closer. I liked the feel of his body. It was hard but resilient, like a dog's head.

"Spring in this neighborhood means slush. Slush on the streets. Slush dripping from the buildings. Slush on your shoes."

"And slush all over Molson," he contributed.

"Particularly that. Molson becomes one enormous

129

slushball. He just rolls down the street and all you can see are his eyes and his paws."

"There's not much we can do about it. It comes every year—like it or not."

"You can do something about it," I said.

"What?"

"I don't know. A hotshot powerful developer like you . . . can't you just order spring away . . . evict it . . . like you would when clearing out an SRO hotel?"

"I'll try," he said, playing along uncomfortably with the joke.

"Good. After all—what are powerful friends for?"

He laughed and kissed me. Bernstein suddenly appeared over us and stared down.

"What does he want?" Patrice asked nervously.

"He wants to make sure we don't make love again."

"Jealousy?"

"No, he doesn't like noise."

"What does Bernstein like?"

"Morphine."

"Morphine?" He was startled.

"And sardines."

I was very close to disclosing the strange events surrounding the Church of the Homeless but I restrained myself. It was hard. I wanted very much to brag about Bernstein.

"I'm kidding you," I said.

"Well, stop kidding for a minute. I have a favor to ask you."

"Want to borrow money?" I teased.

"No. I want to borrow you for an evening."

"But you have me."

"I want you to come to a birthday party with me this Sunday afternoon."

"Your ex-wife's?"

"No. The mayor's."

I stared at him in horror.

130

"Are you serious?"

"Quite serious."

"There is not enough money in this world to get me to celebrate the birthday of the mayor of this city. Nothing . . . there is absolutely nothing that would be able to get me to participate . . . not even a contract to play Lady Macbeth in a Peter Brook production at the Drury Lane Theatre."

"Yes. I understand you don't like the man. But this is a favor for me. It's a combination fund-raiser and party at the Sheraton."

"Why don't you just send him a check?"

"I have to be there. I have to see some people who will be there. And I want you with me."

"Why?"

"Because"—he paused and thought a while before finishing his thought—"because we're part of each other."

It was a silly description but oddly touching. I understood what he meant.

Patrice had never really asked for anything before. I had to think. On the one hand it was truly a banal favor in spite of my loathing for the mayor and all that he represented—all I had to do was sit for a few hours and play the smart, pretty consort with people I despised. Hell, I did it all the time as a cashier in restaurants.

On the other hand, it was another step in the progression . . . his perhaps unconscious desire to get me into his world.

I decided to go with him. My reasoning was not subtle. He had been very good to me. He had been, oddly enough, a perfect lover—if such an animal existed—asking little . . . suffering well my lack of intensity . . . attempting to avoid all conversations and actions that would nail me to the relationship. He loved me. I knew that. It was a payback.

"I'll go this once," I said.

"Thank you."

I turned away from him and stared at the large windows. I was going to the mayor's birthday party. Where was Mrs. Toast going?

He picked me up that Sunday at three in the afternoon. It was a warmish, wettish late winter day. No sun.

I wore a brown sweater and a checked skirt with my mother's pale necklace—underneath my parka.

Patrice frowned when he saw the parka but brightened when he saw what was underneath. The parka would be checked at the door. He was wearing a beautiful new tweed sports jacket, a red flannel shirt, and a dark tie. He looked like one of those movie directors about to accept an award at the Cannes Film Festival.

This particular Sheraton hotel straddles 52nd Street and Seventh Avenue like a grotesque wounded albatross—white and huge.

We entered on Seventh and were ushered into a lounge where drinks were being served. Many people greeted Patrice. He introduced me simply as his friend, Sally Tepper. I saw the large domed head of the mayor against one wall.

It was truly the first time I had ever seen Patrice operating in his professional milieu. And he was operating. He was charming, incisive, witty, always to the point. He seemed to be selecting targets at random, but I could feel an intelligence at work. It was as if he were saying to himself: "I'll spend two minutes with A. Three minutes with B. Thirty seconds with C."

I had known that real estate developers in a city like New York—and particularly in a neighborhood like Hell's Kitchen—live or die on their relationships with politicians, with the whole range of elected and appointed officials who have the power to open or close the sluice gates. I was just not prepared for Patrice's act. Anyway, he was brilliant.

When it was obvious that everyone had enough alcohol

in one form or another and the level of polite conversation had escalated to a sort of dull roar, we were escorted out of the lounge and into a much larger room.

It was, in fact, breathtakingly gaudy. A long raised dais was along one wall. The mayor and his entourage filed across it and sat. Above were bright birthday decorations that looked as if they had been produced by a refugee from a Chinese New Year's celebration.

An enormous, semicircular buffet table was on the other side, filled with an astonishing array of food—everything from nouvelle cuisine to baked sturgeon. Twenty tables were scattered throughout the room. Eight settings were on each table.

It took me a while to figure out the procedure. There was no formal seating arrangement or place cards. And one didn't pick up the food oneself, even though it was an open buffet. Two waiters were assigned to each table. They told the guests what kind of dishes were available and then brought the food from the buffet.

The table Patrice selected filled quickly. The couple next to us was introduced to me as Louis and Donna Fried. They were lawyers, obviously well-connected politically, and they seemed to know Patrice quite well. In fact, they were charming.

Donna Fried, as she was about to take a tidbit off the dish of radiccio and salmon, which had been brought to the table by one of the waiters, said, with a kindly twinkle: "You're younger than his last one."

"Who was his last one?" I asked, really knowing absolutely nothing about Patrice's love life in the past.

"He was courting a woman who could get him a zoning variance."

We all laughed, even Patrice, although he did look a bit uncomfortable.

One of the waiters put down a large bowl of green salad in front of Louis Fried, who said: "I don't want that.

I wanted some pasta salad." The waiter apologized and spilled half the salad on the table pulling it away. He was obviously incompetent.

"And then," Donna continued, "there was the Mexican woman. Did you tell Sally about the Mexican woman, Stephen?"

It was odd hearing someone call Patrice by his first name. I never had and I was sleeping with him.

"She was a sculptress," Patrice said to me, as if that explained something.

Then Donna launched into a very funny and very filthy analysis of the relationships at a nearby table. I didn't even know who she was talking about and I almost fell off my chair laughing. Her husband added a few choice tidbits. They were like a well-rehearsed song and dance team.

The incompetent waiter plopped a small plate of mozzarella cheese and sliced tomatoes in front of me. I explained to him that I hadn't ordered it and didn't want it. He apologized and looked around, obviously trying to remember who had ordered it.

As the waiter moved to the next table, I realized that I had seen him somewhere before.

I knew that waiter.

He was tall, thin, with very bad posture. He had a shock of unruly light brown hair and a large hawklike nose.

He was probably an out-of-work actor, I realized—most of them were.

I tried very hard to remember where I knew him from as the Frieds opened a dialogue with another couple at the table. Had he been in one of my acting classes? In a workshop production? Had he worked in one of the restaurants I had cashiered in?

Maybe from the neighborhood? From Amy's? The laundromat? A friend of a friend?

It was no use. I couldn't place him.

There was some movement on the dais. Obviously, the

formal party was about to begin—the speeches and the tributes. The waiters began to clear away the dishes. I realized that there would be no coffee until after the speeches.

"Now," Patrice said, opening his jacket and leaning back on his chair, "the trick is to go to sleep while keeping one's eyes open until the speeches are finished."

"When do we sing *Happy Birthday?*"

"At the end. When they wheel the cake out."

Patrice looked at ease, prosperous, in control. He had, as usual, eaten very lightly. He leaned over and exchanged a private joke with Louis Fried. Then he leaned back and kissed me quickly on the side of my head. It was an unusual display of public affection for him. I wondered if he had drunk too much.

Someone on the dais was banging a spoon on a plate for order.

Patrice whispered in my ear: "Someone ought to tell that idiot he's not going to be called up for a speech."

He was pointing to the bumbling waiter, who was standing right in the center of the room staring absurdly at the Mayor's birthday decorations over the dais.

Then the waiter turned and started back to our table.

Patrice started to say something else, but he stopped and his grip tightened.

"My God!" Patrice's voice was desperate, almost gurgled.

I stared at him, concerned, thinking he was ill. His fingers were pointing toward the approaching waiter.

I turned. The waiter was only two or three feet away.

Right then, I knew who he was.

He had shaved his scraggly beard and moustache. He had cut his hair. He had cleaned up. He looked totally different.

But it was Arthur—one of Charlie Seven's family. It was Arthur—whom Digger and I had been looking for, along with Sleepy, the last two of Charlie Seven's family who had not been located.

Yes, it was Arthur. But what the hell was he doing in the Sheraton?

I didn't have time to greet him. Because a second later he was standing right beside me, a gun in his hand, pressed against the side of my head.

I stayed absolutely still. I heard yells and then shouts and then shuffling of feet and chairs. Then silence, except for the close presence of Arthur's body . . . a kind of rasping . . . breathing.

I had never been so frightened in my life. I had never been so confused.

"Do you want her to die, Patrice? Do you want her to die?"

Arthur screamed his question out. The gun pressed harder against my head.

I heard Patrice reply: "Put the gun down, Arthur. Don't do anything stupid." His voice sounded miles away.

I didn't understand how Patrice knew the derelict's name, but it made me feel better . . . it got the trembling under control.

"Arthur, it's me, Sally, Charlie Seven's friend. Don't you remember me? I used to bring you food," I whispered to him, my voice cracking. He ignored me.

"Get out of the chair, Patrice," Arthur ordered.

I could hear Patrice stand up.

"That's right. Stand right there, Patrice. Stand right up."

"Put the gun away," I heard Patrice say.

"Shut up, Patrice! I want everyone to look at you. I want the Mayor and all these beautiful people to look at you.

"They think you're wonderful, Patrice . . . but they don't know who you are, do they?"

Arthur was speaking in short violent bursts, his chest heaving, his gun hand shaky against my head.

"But I know who you are. You buy our wine. You give us money to burn down the houses. Don't you?

"And you paid me and Little Arthur to kill Charlie Seven. Didn't you? Because he didn't want to do it anymore. Because Charlie got religion.

"And then Little Arthur killed himself because he loved Charlie Seven! We all loved Charlie Seven. But you didn't love him, Patrice. No, you didn't."

What he said sickened me. The gun at my head seemed to lose all significance. My insides were crumbling. Arthur's ranting was that of a madman—but there wasn't one word I disbelieved. It was impossible not to believe.

My lover had murdered my friend . . . Molson's friend.

"Tell the fucking truth, Patrice," Arthur screamed, "tell the truth to all these fat people."

There was no response from Patrice.

I heard Arthur cock the gun.

"Tell the truth, Patrice," he screamed again.

I closed my eyes. For some strange reason all I could think was where in my skull the bullet would enter.

I heard three shots.

No bullet entered me.

They entered Arthur—penetrating his neck. They were fired by a plainclothes cop assigned to the Mayor.

I remained seated, oddly calm . . . oddly reflective.

Arthur's blood was all over me—sweet, smelly, sticky, warm.

Arthur was on the floor.

I saw Donna Fried on the floor beside him, holding an elegantly embossed Sheraton cloth napkin against the spurting wound in his neck. He was alive. His legs thrashed.

They loaded him onto a portable stretcher and wheeled him away in minutes.

Patrice sat down on the chair next to me.

I stared at him.

He took a napkin and dabbed at my face and clothes—just as Donna had done with Arthur.

I picked up a water glass from the table and smashed it against the side of his face.

18

Patrice called me twenty-four hours later. I picked up the phone. I held it. I didn't return the greeting. I was silent.

"I look like Quasimodo," he said. "They put twenty-six stitches in my face. I told the police it was accidental. You were distraught from being a hostage. You just swung the glass. You didn't know what you were doing."

I remained silent. I felt nothing for him but a cold, absolute hatred. All I could think of in relation to his voice was Charlie Seven, hanging in the subway station—Patrice's legacy.

Then he said, very quietly: "I swear to you, Sally, that not one word that madman said was true. Sure, I knew him. He and his friends used to clean out basements for me for wine money. I never paid them to torch anything. I never torched a building in my life."

He waited. I didn't respond.

"Sally, are you there? Sally, talk to me."

I was silent. His voice was rising.

"I didn't know Charlie Seven, Sally. I never paid anyone to burn houses. I never paid anyone to hurt anyone."

I hung up the phone, grabbed Heineken, and hugged him.

His call had confused me. For the first time since the horrid events at the Sheraton the possibility surfaced that Patrice was telling the truth. Was it plausible? Was it possible that Arthur was lying or deranged? Who was lying? Who was crazy?

I had the shakes. That gun against my head was beginning to finish its job twenty-four hours after it had been removed.

The phone rang again.

I let it ring—five times, ten times, fifteen times; on the thirty-first ring I picked it up.

It was Patrice again.

"Please don't hang up on me," he pleaded, "don't hang up."

I held the phone. He was breathing heavily, almost panting. I closed my eyes. The fact that I had cut his face no longer gave me any pleasure. I stared at the mattress on which we had made love so many times, most of it good. Confusion. So much confusion. His body and mine had been wrapped together. We had spent nights together. We had touched and tasted each other.

The voice on the phone began to talk.

"Don't believe that insane street wino, Sally. I am telling you the truth. Maybe he hates me. Maybe a lot of people hate me. But Sally, I'm not a murderer. I'm not an arsonist. I love you, Sally. I won't lie to you. I can't lie to you."

There was silence. A long silence. Again that exhaustion and panting on the other end of the line.

I hung the phone up very gently. I began to pace. His calls were continuing to destroy my confidence in his guilt.

140

I made a cup of coffee and ate a piece of whole wheat bread with a slice of Port Salut on it.

Arthur's story must be corroborated, I realized. It was owed to Patrice. It was another payback that was due to him.

But who could affirm it? Who could deny it? Only someone close to Charlie Seven.

Only Mrs. Toast.

My logic was impeccable. My grasp of reality, however, was woefully thin.

Mrs. Toast had never told me anything rational; she had never disclosed anything to me before she entered Allissandro's bizarre Church of the Homeless; she was uncommunicative while she was in that church, and she would no doubt be just as distant and cryptic now that the church was disbanded and she was back on the street, as crazy as she always was.

But, I reasoned, perhaps Mrs. Toast would be more forthcoming now. Perhaps she would make an effort to make herself understood, to break out of her lunatic torpor.

I realized that everything had changed now.

Mrs. Toast was out on the street without her armor, without her white shirt, without her family.

And she was probably addicted to morphine.

I began to scheme feverishly. I could go down to the subway tunnel again and get some morphine syrettes. Or get them from Digger. I was sure he had pocketed some when he was down there, no matter how much I had protested against the idea.

Then I could make a trade with Mrs. Toast.

Some goodies to ease her craving in return for what she really knew about Charlie Seven and Patrice and the arson and the murder.

I had already put my boots on to leave the loft and search for Digger when the depravity of my scheme finally hit me.

My god! I was going to torture Mrs. Toast. I was going to shove morphine under a decent old woman's nose so she would crumble and beg and talk!

Suddenly I realized how ingenious that pig Patrice had been with his telephone calls.

He was counting on the fact that when it came down to brass tacks I would identify with him and all he represented—not with a derelict like Arthur.

He was manipulating me. He was squeezing me. He was depending on the fact that in spite of her do-gooder social conscience, old Sally Tepper was just another hard-pressed middle-class lady who wouldn't jeopardize her new loft, or her new lover, or anything else really, for a crazed drifter.

He was counting on the fact that I wanted to believe him and not Arthur. And that I would.

I almost had. My shame made me nauseated. I threw up the cheese and bread.

Then I stormed out of the loft and headed north to Roosevelt Hospital.

I was out of my head with shame and rage at what I had almost done. My heart was filled with prayers for Arthur's recovery. Please God, let him live. Please God, let him testify. Please God, let him send that son of a bitch Patrice away forever.

I knew in my head, of course, that if Arthur survived, and testified, it would never stand up in court; if, indeed, there was even an indictment. But my heart was something else. This whole thing . . . this conflict between head and heart didn't really mean a damn.

When I got to Roosevelt Hospital, a woman in starched white trousers and a name tag that read ALVAREZ told me Arthur had died an hour ago.

"Are you a relative?" she asked, no doubt looking for someone to relieve them of the body.

"No," I said, walked outside, and threw up once again, this time on the brick wall outside the emergency ward.

19

Spring finally did come in all its slushiness. I was totally isolated—no work, no parts, no friends. The idea of even looking at Patrice made me physically ill. As for Beth and Allissandro, once in a while I saw them on the street but they avoided me. Why not? I had ruined their lunatic vision. They were back in the real and ugly world of Christian love—scrounging food, money, medical help.

It was inevitable that I would drift toward Digger. And I did. Oh, there was no sex in it, nor was it a deeply felt friendship. It was merely that neither of us had anywhere else to go for the time being. We were just hanging out, in the old-fashioned sense.

I didn't see him every day. But a couple of afternoons a week we would go for a long walk together and then sit and sip ale in one of those seedy Hell's Kitchen bars that survived only because they enticed drinkers inside with incredibly low prices on hot plate specials such as brisket with carrots, peas, and mashed potatoes.

Digger enjoyed entering those kinds of bars with a tall, good-looking, older redhead on his arm; he enjoyed people in bars thinking I was his woman, his wife, his hooker—anything. It was a harmless fantasy; it didn't bother me at all.

Then, after the bar, we would go to one of the cheap ethnic restaurants on Ninth Avenue—either Italian or Greek or Afghan or Chinese or West Indian—and eat well. Then we would go our separate ways—me to the dogs and a night of reading and fantasizing, and Digger, I suppose, to steal.

One early April afternoon, I decided on a whim to deplete my bank account by one-third and take Digger to a nice restaurant and bar. I was feeling better and about to dip my toe back into the world. I had even applied for a cashier's job at a new restaurant on 47th Street, just west of Eighth. I wanted to show my appreciation to Digger for his company.

We walked to 57th Street and then all the way east to the small park on the East River. Then we went into one of those posh bars that are chock full of Citibank executives.

The hostess didn't know what to make of us—we looked like a showgirl and a junkie, I suppose.

We ordered the entire menu—drinks, not ale this time, appetizer, main course, salad, dessert, brandy, coffee—the works.

But Digger wasn't happy. He was eating almost reluctantly. The voices from the other tables seemed to be grating on him.

"You like it better on the West Side?" I asked. It was a patronizing question.

"Ain't this the West Side?" he asked in mock astonishment.

"Eat your swordfish," I said. Digger had ordered it

because he had, odd as it may seem, never eaten swordfish in his life. Maybe he thought it would be served with the sword intact.

He put the fork down. "You don't talk anymore about what I should do," he said.

I didn't understand what he was talking about.

"C'mon," he exploded in a fury, "I'm talking about me becoming an actor."

I just laughed out loud. I couldn't help it. I had forgotten all about it. My laughter insulted him. He looked as if he was about to throw the swordfish at me.

"Digger, I didn't know you were serious about that."

"Bullshit! You just don't think I can make it as an actor."

"Digger, I don't have any idea whether you'd be a good actor or not. And besides, being good doesn't have anything to do with making it."

"Well, how do I start? How do I find out?"

"But why do you want to be an actor? I mean, there are three million actors in New York and only a hundred and twelve of them are working at any one time."

"What I do is easy?"

He had a point. I would rather be an actor than a thief.

"You want to be an actor? Go to acting school. Scrape together a couple of hundred dollars and take the plunge."

"I don't like your attitude."

"Digger, what do you want me to say?" He was, truly, an adolescent.

"Something about me as an actor. Something about what you think."

He was asking me, I think, to judge him as a man or as a human being.

"Digger, it's no big deal being an actor. Actors aren't heroes, Digger. They're pathetic hustlers, just like me. The script is the hero. The stage is the hero. But not the actor."

"Then why the hell are you in it?"

"Well, I went into it for the same reason you might go into it—a romantic reason, I guess."

His lips curled in scorn.

"Digger, look, I love acting. But it's just another craft . . . another job . . . another way to starve."

"That's not what I hear."

"From who?"

"I got my sources."

"It's what you want to be, obviously."

"What school should I go to?"

"I'll make some calls if you're really serious."

"You think I'm not serious?"

"I don't know what to think."

"You know, Sally, I'm tired of taking your shit. Like you know it all."

"Relax, Digger, you're getting all excited for no reason."

We finished the meal. He remained silent, muttering and glaring at me.

When we got outside he exploded again in a fury, accusing me of all sorts of petty crimes, insults, and god knows what else.

I started to walk west. He kept a step behind me. He kept peppering me with accusations.

"You don't think I'm handsome enough to be an actor. You think my complexion is too lousy."

"You don't think I'm smart enough to be an actor."

"You don't think I read."

"You don't think I have guts enough to be an actor."

Poor Digger. The movies had rotted his head. He really thought Clint Eastwood was brave.

When we reached Fifth Avenue he had exhausted his list of accusations and shut his mouth.

To cheer him up, to heal the sudden absurd gulf between us, I took him into one of *his* bars. The lunch crowd was gone. We sat in a booth and shared a bottle of Bass ale. We stared at each other. And finally we both broke up with laughter. He apologized in his fashion. God—what

146

a long winter it had been! Love betrayed. Intelligence questioned. Friends murdered. Neighborhood gone insane. New churches. New drugs. Oh, what a winter it had been. We held hands.

"It's better than the 'D' train," he joked.

When we left the bar it was obvious both of us had drunk too much and mixed too many drinks.

I invited him back to the loft. Once there, he collapsed on the sofa, so wiped out he even ignored the dogs' pleas for cheese, and fell fast asleep.

I lay down on the mattress and was out in seconds.

It was my name that awoke me. I sat up. It was pitch dark. I had been asleep for hours. Digger was still asleep on the sofa. But it wasn't Digger who was calling my name.

Was it a dream? I flicked on a light.

I heard it again—louder. Someone was calling my name from outside the door.

I opened the door without thinking. It sounded like the super.

An enormous man was standing outside. He was wearing a flannel shirt—red and white. He was wearing a pair of carpenter's jeans. He was wearing large, high, incredibly filthy boots.

I stared at him blankly. His face was odd. There were white marks over the top third of his face and his eyelids. They gave the impression that his eyes were closed. His face was fat. He wore no hat. Wisps of hair stood up on his head.

"Don't you know me, Sally?" he asked.

I stepped back, confused, and then realized with a tremendous burst of joy that it was Sleepy—the last one of Charlie Seven's family who had been missing.

"Sleepy!" I almost screamed his name and flung my arms around him.

"Can I stay here for a few hours? I'm in trouble. My stuff is downstairs."

"Of course, stay as long as you want."

He disengaged from my embrace and went down to collect his stuff. I left the door open and went back into the loft.

Digger was up, sitting on the sofa, trying to light a cigarette. He looked as if he had a terrible hangover.

"Digger," I said happily, tousling his hair, "Sleepy is alive and well."

"Who the hell is Sleepy?" he asked.

"One of the people you were supposed to find for me."

"Wonderful," he said, sardonically.

"Sally."

Sleepy was calling me from just inside the door. He didn't have any luggage or bags. All he had was what looked like two large whiskey bottles—one in each hand.

There was something odd about the bottles . . . the tip of each seemed to be lit with a kind of candle.

I heard Digger scream at me to get down.

I saw Sleepy fling the bottles.

Then I felt an enormous whoosh of heat and orange flames seemed to leap out of the walls.

20

It could have been worse, much worse. We could have been roasted. Like that guy with the chestnuts on Eighth Avenue in the winter."

One of Sleepy's firebombs had broken against the sofa. The other had slammed into a wall. Because the loft was in an industrial building, the floors and walls were concrete and brick. All flames did was sear them.

The sofa had gone up in flames but Digger and I had somehow gotten the fire out with blankets and water and emptying whatever liquids we had in the refrigerator on it—soda, beer, milk, orange juice.

The windows were still open, but the choking stench was still in the loft. The dogs huddled under a far window—all of them still frightened, all of them blinking.

"Weird friends you got," Digger said.

It had all happened so fast. It was all so crazy.

Digger noted: "If he had hit your big closet with one of those firebombs, it would have done the job."

He began to pull away the charred fabric of the sofa to make sure there were no smoldering hot spots.

I sat down on the floor. The firebombing seemed to have happened months ago, but I was sitting on a wet floor, drenched from what we had poured on the fire only a short time ago.

The dogs were starting to move toward me, tentatively. We could all have died horribly, I realized. All of us.

Why had Sleepy wanted us to die? Why would he try to murder us all? What had I ever done to Sleepy except try to make his miserable life a little less so. It was the last straw in a winter of betrayal. I would not turn the other cheek anymore.

"Digger, can you get me a gun?"

"A gun?"

"Right."

"I got you a gun a year ago. Don't you remember?"

"I don't have it anymore."

"Why do you need it?"

"For Sleepy . . . to find Sleepy . . . to make sure Sleepy doesn't hurt my dogs."

"Sally, I think you ought to go to the cops. That Church of Loonies getting high off the 'D' train was one thing—but this guy is serious."

"No cops, Digger. The only thing cops ever did for me is evict me. Just you, me, and a gun."

"I don't have the contacts anymore to get a gun."

"Can't you buy one on the street for me? I'll give you the money in the morning."

"Anyway—you couldn't find Sleepy before. How you gonna find him now?"

"Just get me the gun."

"I can get you a sawed-off shotgun."

"Can I work it?"

"All guns are the same, Sally. Just pull the trigger. Two triggers. Two barrels. Many holes. It's heavy and ugly, but it works."

"I'm cleaning out my bank account in the morning. Get me the gun, Digger. What's left, you can have."

"You're hiring me again?"

"Right."

Three of the dogs were now nuzzling me. Budweiser still had the shakes and her nose was hot and dry.

"Get me the gun, Digger." Everything was calm now and clear. I was about to become powerful, and it was only power that would enable me to save what had to be saved—the dogs, me, Digger, what life I had. I wasn't going to be snuffed out.

The dogs and I all slept together on the mattress. A spring breeze from the river purged the loft. When I awoke in the morning the stench had gone—only the stains and scars remained.

Digger came back at 9:30 the next morning, carrying an old suitcase.

He laid the suitcase on the kitchen table and opened it. The gun was wrapped in a bath towel, which he unrolled.

It was the ugliest thing I had ever seen in my life: brutish, blunt, dull, thick.

Digger picked it up and showed me how to break it open, load the shells, snap it shut, cock it. Once, twice, three times he showed me. Then I did it myself and rewrapped it in the towel.

I made us black coffee—all the milk had been used to drench the sofa.

"So, you got your gun, Sally."

"Thank you."

"Any time, if you pay. Now what do we do?"

"Find Sleepy."

"Where?"

I sipped the coffee.

"I don't know where yet. But I think I can figure it out."

"Sure, like you found all the others."

I ignored his sarcasm.

"Digger, did you see how Sleepy was dressed?"

"No, I only saw him for a second—at the door—before he threw the Molotov cocktails."

"Did you see his boots?"

"No."

"They were those high boots, that sewer workers use— up to just below the knee."

"So what?"

"It wasn't the boots, Digger. A lot of people who don't work in sewers wear them. It was what was on the boots."

"Yeah?"

"They were filthy, really caked."

"So what? A lot of mud on the street."

"No, Digger. Pigeon and gull droppings. That's what it was. And pieces of feathers."

"So what? This city floats on pigeon shit. Hell, this neighborhood is the pigeon capital of the world."

"Digger, did you ever work in one of those big old industrial buildings on Tenth or Eleventh Avenues? They tore down a lot of them, some were renovated into co-ops . . . but a few are still left."

"Once or twice. I worked at a printing plant in one of those buildings when I was a kid, after school. I used to sweep up."

"How high up was it? What floor?"

"I don't remember. Tenth floor maybe."

"I used to work in the office of a metal extruder in one of those buildings. It was on Forty-Ninth, I think, between Eleventh and Twelfth. The office was high up with enormous windows. We had to make sure that we closed the windows each night—because if we didn't, when we came in the next morning the floors would be littered with pigeon droppings and feathers."

"Why feathers?"

"Because the pigeons nested on the ledges and their nests were full of molting feathers. The wind kept blowing all of it into the building."

"Yeah but, Sally, do you know how many buildings like that are still in Hell's Kitchen? I mean, it'll take years searching them."

"Wait, Digger. We can narrow it."

"How?"

"He has to be staying in an abandoned building— broken windows, sloshed over with pigeon droppings, feathers, water. Right?"

"But how do we find abandoned buildings?"

"We look for them."

"You mean just walk around and look for them?"

Digger was getting very uncomfortable.

"That's what I mean. You and I take a walk. Up Ninth Avenue. Down Tenth Avenue. Up Eleventh Avenue. Down Twelfth Avenue."

He groaned. He cursed. He stalled. But then we started out, leaving the dogs home.

By late that afternoon we had located only four. Two were on 53rd Street between Tenth and Eleventh. One was on 46th, just east of Twelfth. And the last one was on the corner of Eleventh Avenue and 44th Street.

They were empty, desolate boxes, the windows long broken or shattered.

I named the buildings with letters—L,M,N,O.

We entered L first, that very afternoon, carrying the shotgun in a dancer's bag. It was a nine-story building. The front was boarded up, but there were five holes in the wood, each one large enough to accommodate a very fat man.

We climbed through and started up the stairwell. I was frightened. Digger was tense. If we were stopped by someone or seen by someone, they would call the police and they might look in the dancer's bag. They wouldn't find a leotard.

"If he's here," I said to Digger, "figure the last three floors."

We left the stairwell at the seventh floor, out of breath. Digger kicked a rusted metal door open. It was a filthy cold space that had once obviously held linotype machines.

Digger's flashlight illuminated the floor.

"You were right, Sally," he whispered appreciatively, "look at the mess."

The perimeter of the floor by the broken windows were indeed coated with pigeon droppings and feathers and a lot else that was simply not identifiable.

On the next floor all we found were rats—large and powerful—running along the overhead pipes.

On the last floor we found thousands of rotted crates that had once held some kind of imported dinnerware.

We covered building M next. Nothing.

The day after we covered N and O. We went early and searched them thoroughly, looking for some sign of Sleepy, some mark he had left, a bag he had thrown away, a paper he had read, an apple he had munched—anything. But Sleepy or any part or any residue of him was not to be found.

"Well, it sounded logical when you said it, but so did all that stuff about the 'D' train." Digger had lost heart.

By the end of the week we had dug up four more abandoned industrial buildings in Hell's Kitchen. We visited each, shotgun in tow, looking for Sleepy . . . anticipating Sleepy . . . but he was not there.

"You don't mind if I take the weekend off, do you?" Digger asked on a Friday afternoon.

I didn't answer immediately. I had become increasingly nervous about staying alone in the loft at night. The shotgun helped, the dogs were there, of course, but the fear of another firebomb attack was always present. I had the distinct feeling that if I did not find Sleepy he would find me . . . and if I did not in some way kill him or his hatred, he would kill me.

Digger persisted: "C'mon, Boss, give me a break. I mean, now that we're in the real estate inspection business, I gotta work regular hours."

"Sure, Digger, take the weekend off. But do me a favor. Give me a number I can reach you at. If something comes up, like a firebomb, I don't want to have to run from bodega to bodega leaving messages for you."

He wrote a number on a piece of paper and handed it to me, grinning.

"My cousin," he said, "I'm staying with my cousin."

Digger always constructed fantasy relatives to cover up something else. He was always introducing a cousin or an uncle into the conversation. I doubted their existence.

After he left I once again started cleaning up in the wake of the fire. But I tired of it quickly and started to brush the dogs instead. They milled around me, howling and jostling each other, trying to get a stroke of the wire brush. I could never understand why brushing drove my dogs into such a frenzy. They seemed to love it and hate it at the same time. Their behavior would range from rolling on their backs in a seeming ecstasy to snapping, snarling attempts to bite the brush out of my hand.

I must have brushed them literally for hours; I brushed them until I and they were exhausted.

Then I lay down on the mattress and fell asleep for about an hour, only to be wakened by a sound—a scraping sound. Was it from the door? I was so frightened that I temporarily forgot where I had placed the shotgun. When I saw the dancer's bag I rushed to it, fumbling with the zipper, but finally extracting the ugly weapon and loading it.

I waited, crouched, my eyes on the door. I was drenched with sweat. The fear of another firebombing made me so weak that I doubted if I could pull the trigger even if I wanted to.

Then the sound came again. It was from the street, not from the stairs. It was the sound of a garbage truck starting up its grinder. I relaxed, feeling like an absolute idiot. But the fear had a lock on my brain. Death by fire has always had a special terror for me. Sleepy was out there—somewhere. He wanted to kill me for reasons I did not know. He was outside the network of logic and control to which other people subscribed. He had no mercy and one had the feeling that nothing would prevent him from trying again until I and all my dogs were shadows on the floor.

The clock read 12:20 AM. It was going to be a long night. I would not get to sleep again easily.

I walked to one of the windows and sat on the ledge. Heineken inspected me.

"What's the matter with you?" I asked.

He moved away. I knew that my fear had intensified because I had been sure Sleepy would be found—and he was not found. His boots were, I believed, a map of his travels. I knew the neighborhood well; it was my avocation. It was only in those kinds of abandoned buildings that he could have decorated his boots with such a telltale covering.

I stared down into the street. No one was walking. It was obvious to me that I had missed something again; that there was a serious flaw in my reasoning.

I looked at the door to the loft, then closed my eyes, trying to recapture the sequence of events. I had heard my name called. I had opened the door. Why had I opened the door without asking who it was? Because I was dopey from sleep. Or perhaps because Digger was there and I felt safe. But I still would have opened the door for Sleepy if I had known it was him. I wanted him safe. I had been worried about him. I had paid Digger to look for him as well as the others after Charlie Seven's murder.

What about his clothes? His speech? Had I missed anything?

Only his boots had revealed something—and I had acted on that without success.

I visualized once again those filthy boots: a necklace of pigeon and gull droppings and feathers around each boot, like an identification bracelet in a hospital.

I stood up, tense, then sat down on the ledge. Something in my revisualization jarred me. Or was it how I had explained the boots to Digger? Or was it something else?

I went back through my cluttered memory to the abandoned buildings we had searched so futilely. That was what was bothering me—those buildings.

They all had something in common. Yes, they were all littered with pigeon droppings and feathers.

But they had something else in common. There were no gull nests or droppings in any of those buildings!

The banal simplicity of it startled me. Gulls don't nest in those buildings. Pigeons do. Every Hell's Kitchen kid knows that.

Gulls nest, when they do, near the river pilings.

I walked quickly to the phone, picked it up, then put it down again. I had to call Digger. I knew exactly the mistake I had made—no gulls.

I knew exactly where Sleepy would be hiding among the pigeons and the gulls.

I was like an excited adolescent. I hugged myself.

Sleepy was staying at the old abandoned Marine Terminal that lay like a beached whale jutting out into the Hudson at the foot of West 57th Street.

It had been a landmark in Hell's Kitchen for decades; an ugly hulk that was populated by pigeons and gulls and feral cats and water rats and dead bodies dumped by mythical mobsters.

It used to be the traditional target of Hell's Kitchen children before it became too unstable and dangerous. Rocks, BB pellets, slingshots were heaved and fired at it year after year until not a single one of the literally thousands of windows remained.

157

He was there, I knew. If he was still in Hell's Kitchen, he was there.

I dialed the number Digger had given me—his "cousin."

A girl answered. I asked for Digger. She said he had stepped out. I told her it was an emergency. She repeated he had stepped out. She asked what I wanted.

"Tell Digger to meet me in the old Marine Terminal at Fifty-seventh and the river."

"You mean when he comes back?"

"Yes."

"But it's almost one o'clock in the morning."

"Just tell him."

I hung up the phone. I took the shotgun out of the bag and loaded it, then wrapped it in a newspaper. I couldn't wait for Digger. He might never get the message.

Taking my two largest dogs, Molson and Bernstein, I left the loft and walked north on Eleventh until I reached 57th, then one block west across Twelfth, under the elevated West Side Highway, and across the broken paving stones that littered the parking lot in front of the terminal.

It was a warmish night; one could smell the river and hear it lapping against the wooden pilings.

There were no doors left in the terminal, only pieces of hanging rusted metal with huge holes between them— like drapes.

From where I stood, just outside the entrance, I could see inside the massive structure. Moonlight filtered through the roof and made cones of light. This was all that was left of one of the most famous terminals in the world—the one that the newsreels had pictured when the troops came home from all the wars.

For a moment I hesitated. It was not just fear. It was the realization that I might be forced to hurt Sleepy. I didn't want to hurt anyone. I wanted to be left alone.

Then I walked through—holding the dogs on their

leashes with one hand, the flashlight in the other hand, the shotgun under my arm.

The first floor of the enormous structure was covered with a foot of water. Molson was unhappy. Bernstein stoical. We sloshed slowly toward the stairs.

When we climbed to the second floor, a rush of birds exploded up against the walls, their shapes bizarre in the half-light/half-darkness. I froze. Their wings made sounds like gunshots.

I could see little but the twisted frame above and the filth below. Only about an inch of water covered the second floor, but it was slippery and we had to move slowly. There was a terrible stench throughout. Was it life or death? Dying birds or hatching young?

I could hear incessant cooing from the rim of the structure, where the nests were, as if I were being greeted with a chorus of *Silent Night*.

Looking straight ahead I could see the lights of New Jersey, the other side of the Hudson.

I grew dizzy in that ruin from the moonlight, the wetness, the birds. I focused my eyes on the floor and then on what was left of the massive walls, now punched through like Swiss cheese by time and wear.

Only on the uptown side of the terminal did there seem to be solidity.

I moved toward that section, realizing as I approached that a series of huge cargo elevators lined the wall. They looked like giant cubicles, their doors rusted open.

Bernstein suddenly tensed. I could feel it through the leash.

I knelt down beside him, careful not to let my knee reach the water-drenched floor.

What had he heard? What had he sensed? I was afraid to let him off the leash.

I stood up and gave him more of the leash. He moved ahead quickly, pulling me and Molson after him.

When he stopped I realized we had entered one of the cargo elevators—the floor was planked.

I smelled something different. Alcohol. It was alcohol.

I dropped the leashes and grasped the shotgun in one hand, the flashlight in the other. I flicked the light on, running it along the floor.

My eyes caught Sleepy's checked shirt first. He was lying down.

I cocked the shotgun. My heart was pounding against my chest. Had he seen me? What should I do?

I put the light on him again. He didn't move. I edged closer.

When I was only inches away, I had the enormous desire to pull the trigger, to end the threat, to make the gun work.

But Sleepy didn't move or respond in any way. He was stinking, wiped-out drunk. Two bottles of Thunderbird lay against his side. I was looking for a killer and I found a drunk. He couldn't firebomb a hay field in his condition.

The beam of my flashlight moved past him, to the far wall of the elevator, and I swung it from side to side.

There were mailbags stacked along the wall. I stepped over Sleepy and walked to the stacks.

I opened one and shone the light in. No wonder Bernstein had guided us there.

There were hundreds of morphine syrettes in the bag.

Interspersed among them were hastily wrapped stacks of bills—fives, tens, twenties, fastened with rubberbands. It was a great deal of cash.

I went to the next bag.

The same incredible hodgepodge of syrettes and cash. It was mind-boggling even to look at it.

Molson let out a bark. I shushed him severely. He began to whimper. I moved close to him and demanded he shut up.

Then he let out an enormous howl and bounded away.

I ran after him. I saw his rear end vanish in an adjoining cargo elevator.

I stepped inside and shined the light. Molson was pulling at something.

There was a mattress on the floor. And a blanket. Beneath the blanket were two people.

Both of them were naked. They were sitting up, confused, blinking into the light, staring at Molson, who seemed very happy.

One was Beth White.

The other was Charlie Seven.

I covered my eyes for a moment. Then pulled my hand away. I started to speak but couldn't say a word. I started to cry and a second later I was laughing.

How could it be? Charlie Seven was dead, murdered.

I stepped back and looked. It *was* Charlie Seven. Molson was licking his face. Charlie looked exactly the same as I had seen him last, only now he was naked. His body was thin and white, almost like a child's.

Charlie stared at me. I stared back.

Beth covered her nakedness with the blanket. I swung the barrel of the shotgun so it faced the lovers. I had to act. I could not stand there and reason in front of a corpse that had become alive. I had to act.

I cocked the weapon.

"Which of you sent Sleepy to kill me?"

"I sent him," Beth said.

Resurrected Charlie Seven pulled a small bottle of whiskey out from beneath the blanket and guzzled some, as if everything was fine, as if the world was beautiful and clear.

"Why?"

"Because you knew too much and your priorities are no longer in order. You can't be trusted."

"What do I know?"

"About the morphine."

"But you said there was only one cache."

"I lied. That's what Allissandro thought. Just like you thought Charlie was dead because I told you. Even Arthur and Little Arthur, who Patrice hired to beat him up, thought he was dead. They left him hanging because he wouldn't burn any more houses for your true love. But I found him and cut him down because I needed him. And we just hung another body up. There are so many around—aren't there, Sally? In Hell's Kitchen, all derelicts look alike, all die alike, all smell alike."

I moved closer to Charlie Seven. I placed the barrels of the shotgun against his chin and pushed. A savage rope burn circled his neck. It had never healed. He grinned at me and made a face. He kissed Molson on the nose. He sang a little ditty. He seemed to have lost touch with reality. Or had I?

"How many morphine caches are there?"

"There were dozens. But most of them have been emptied; most of the syrettes are right here."

"And you're selling them?"

"Right."

"And you've killed those who tried to rob the caches before you emptied them out?"

"Right."

"And the ones you killed were derelicts because only those people who lived in the subway knew about it?"

"Right."

Her calmness, her clarity, infuriated me.

"Are you insane, Beth? Sitting there naked, with Charlie Seven, and bragging about murder after murder . . . about drug pushing . . . about . . ."

I found it hard to breathe. I found it hard to hold the gun. Molson was lying on his back, being scratched by Charlie Seven.

"Allissandro was a fool," Beth said, "he thought his vision would save the homeless. He truly believed in his vision. But not me. How could one believe in that pathetic sewing circle? What you see here, Sally, is what you can believe in. Only money can save the homeless . . . money to buy buildings in Hell's Kitchen . . . money to control how the neighborhood grows . . . and only morphine can provide that money. It is their morphine—they found it. They dug it out. Money from morphine is the only way to beat Patrice and his kind . . . to bury them with money . . . to buy up the buildings they had torched."

She kept pulling at Charlie Seven for support, but he was getting deeper and deeper into his bottle.

Then she sounded on the edge of panic: "What are you going to do, Sally?"

"I'm going to help them put you away, Beth."

"Don't do that, Sally. Don't turn on your friends. Don't destroy the only hope we all have to make this neighborhood a place to live and work and love."

"Love, Beth? Are you insane? You've murdered people up and down the subway system. You're pushing dope. You're firebombing lofts. You're a bandit . . . a killer . . . a warlord, Beth. You can't bring love or justice into this world."

She covered her ears with her hands. Then one hand reached out for Charlie. He pushed it away with a laugh.

Suddenly she was on her feet. Before I could swing the gun back up, she had rushed past me, out of the cargo elevator. She was still naked. She was running fast.

"Beth!" I screamed.

She was running across the floor toward the staircase. She didn't make it. Her feet flew out from under her and she fell hard, sliding along the jagged floor. She screamed as jutting metal cut into her, and then I heard a jangling sound as the floor beneath her seemed to fall away like rotted timbers. There was one final scream, and then I heard the thud of her body striking the floor below.

Charlie called my name for the first time and extended the bottle in friendship.

Holding Bernstein, I crept carefully out on the floor, to where Beth had fallen through. I could see her body crumpled below, grotesquely positioned. One more saint that couldn't make it in Hell's Kitchen.

I crept back, retrieved Molson from a now totally drunk Charlie Seven, and went back into Sleepy's cargo elevator. He was still unconscious.

I laid the shotgun down, tied the dogs' leashes to it, and proceeded to fling the mailbags into the Hudson, one at a time. I heard each one hit the water. I knew the course it would take; I knew the current would bring them out to sea—all of them.

When they were all gone, I wearily traced my steps out of the terminal, leaving the two drunk derelicts to whatever fate they could accommodate. I fell fast asleep, fully clothed, the moment I got back to the loft.

Digger woke me at eleven, banging on the door furiously until I opened.

I was still groggy from sleepy. My neck was stiff. My clothes were clammy.

He pushed past me into the loft.

"Where the hell were you? What the hell happened? I kept calling you when I got the message. I couldn't understand. Something about the Meat Terminal. What's a Meat Terminal, Sally?"

I burst out laughing. "The Marine Terminal, Digger, not the Meat Terminal."

He collapsed on the sofa, shaking his head.

"You meant the old terminal at the river, near Fifty-seventh."

"Right."

"What happened, Sally? Did you find Sleepy?"

"I found Sleepy. And I found Beth White. And I found Charlie Seven in bed with her."

He sat up, startled. "You told me Charlie Seven was dead."

"What I told you and what was the truth are two different things, Digger."

"You're starting to confuse me, Sally. I'm very confused."

I patted him on the head, walked into the kitchen, and began making instant coffee. The dogs had commenced picking on Digger. When I returned with the two cups, Digger was threatening them with the shotgun. It was a new game for the dogs. Molson was licking one of the barrels as if it were candy.

I sat down and very quickly and simply told him what had happened in the Marine Terminal. The recounting of it disturbed me, as if it were slipping rapidly into the distant past and I wanted . . . needed to keep it fresh.

When I finished, he didn't say a word for a long time. Finally, he shook his head sadly and said: "I can't believe you threw all that money and all that morphine into the Hudson River. I can't believe you did that."

"Dirty money, Digger, and dirty dope."

He shook his head with more force, as if he were sitting with a very demented individual—an idiot of the highest order.

"All that money, just lying there," he started to repeat.

He was so upset he gave Molson the whole shotgun. Molson carried it back to his corner and growled when the other dogs approached.

"I have to take a shower, Digger."

"Wait. Do me a favor, Sally. Explain something to me. Was Charlie Seven murdered? Or wasn't he murdered? Who did what to who? The whole thing is like watching a crazy baseball game where everybody is running the bases the wrong way."

"It's Hell's Kitchen, Digger."

"Yeah. I know where I live."

"Listen, Digger. There was this homeless derelict, Charlie Seven, who always needed wine money. So he and two of his friends—Arthur and Little Arthur—used to get it by burning abandoned houses for Stephen Patrice. Then, one day poor Charlie saw the light and joined Allissandro's lunatic Church of the Homeless, and he stopped burning. Patrice was angry. He told Charlie's two friends to straighten him out. They went too far . . . they hung him up and left him for dead.

"But he didn't die, Digger. Beth White found him and cut him down. You see, she, too, wanted Charlie out of the homeless church, and she wanted him alive because she needed help. Beth White was looting dozens of morphine caches established years ago in the 'D' train subway tunnels in case of a nuclear attack. And she was murdering the derelicts who found them to ensure her supply. She humored Allissandro by acting as if she believed in his vision and giving him enough morphine to keep the church going. But she was after much bigger game. She had her own lunatic vision. She was going to *buy* Hell's Kitchen for the homeless. She was going to beat the Stephen Patrices of the world at their own game. And she would do it with the sale of morphine syrettes."

"Was she the one who sent Sleepy to firebomb the loft?"

"Yes. She had to get rid of us, Digger. She couldn't take the chance that one day we would say something about what we found in the subways. She believed I had sold out to the landlords because Patrice and I were lovers. She didn't trust me."

"God save us from ex-nuns," Digger said.

He wasn't drinking his coffee. I had finished mine. I took his cup, also.

"Did you just leave Sleepy and Charlie in the terminal?"

"Yes. They were drunk. They'll be back on the tracks in a few days and they probably won't remember a thing about Beth White or anything. Maybe they were Beth White's hired assassins. Maybe they weren't. We'll never know, really, who pulled the trigger each time. All we know is that Beth had them murdered. She used homeless derelicts to find the morphine. And then she used derelicts to murder the derelicts who found it."

He leaned forward and shook his head.

"What's the matter, Digger?"

"I was just thinking. After all this, there is no way I'll ever step on a 'D' train again."

Molson brought the shotgun back and dropped it in front of us.

"What are you going to do now, Sally?"

"About what?"

"Well, this is Patrice's loft. He'll boot you out."

"I have a lease, Digger."

"You had a lease at the other place, too."

"You don't understand Patrice, Digger. He'll leave me alone. He loves me. He thinks my hatred for him will be fleeting. He doesn't think he did anything very wrong. He thinks burning old buildings is fine because it serves a higher goal. He thinks it was OK to order Charlie Seven beaten. He doesn't think it was his fault that the beating got out of hand. He'll leave me alone for six months and then call me and ask me to have dinner with him."

Digger shrugged. He didn't buy my profile of Patrice. Stout started playing with his shoe. Heineken climbed up on Digger's lap looking for cheese.

"I'm going to be fine, Digger. I'm an actress. I'll be out hustling for parts tomorrow. It's you we should be worried about."

"Me?" Digger exclaimed in mock surprise.

Then he laughed and said: "I'm going to be OK, Sally. I'm a thief. I'll be out hustling for typewriters tomorrow morning."

He was making fun of me in a kindly way.

I finished his coffee. I was very tired, but strangely calm. All, in a sense, was right in Hell's Kitchen. Beth White was in Heaven or Hell. Charlie Seven was back on the street. And all five of my dogs were hungry.

167